D0496236

The Story of Georgia Harvest

Tera Stevens

TATE PUBLISHING
AND ENTERPRISES, LLC

Published by Tate Publishing & Enterprises, LLC
127 E. Trade Center Terrace | Mustang, Oklahoma 73064 USA
1.888.361.9473 | www.tatepublishing.com

Tate Publishing is committed to excellence in the publishing industry. The company reflects the philosophy established by the founders, based on Psalm 68:11,
"The Lord gave the word and great was the company of those who published it."

Book design copyright © 2014 by Tate Publishing, LLC. All rights reserved.
Cover design by Allen Jomoc
Interior design by Joana Quilantang

Published in the United States of America

ISBN: 978-1-62994-369-5
Fiction / Romance / General
13.11.26

To gram, your travels have inspired me more than you know. To Herman your positivity and love kept me motivated, I could not have done this without you. To my siblings, the skies are limitless do whatever your heart desires.

Acknowledgement

Tate Publishing

Bud Rogers

Chapter 1

At this point in my life I only searched for a defi-nition, a hope, clarity, some hint to where, what, when I would find myself and know my purpose. Every morning I would wake up, hit snooze on my phone, and pull the hideous yellow sheets (which matched nothing in my bedroom) overtop of my tousled dark hair. After my alarm rang three more times, I hit dismiss and like a zombie tossed my petite body off my mattress and on to the cool wooden floor. I was in a hurry every morning. I prepared for nothing. I would throw together an outfit, messily throw my hair up, grab for a dried-out mascara wand, and run down the black metal staircase outside of my window, always in hopes to avoid the landlord, who I was currently indebted to for some three months' rent.

I hated my job, which I couldn't even say paid the bills, as most nonsensical adults made the excuse to defend themselves being failures and not completing their dreams of veterinarians or rock stars. I worked a desk job in my step-aunt's office. I was the lady who would call you every week and ask if you were inter-ested in buying miscellaneous items that you had no need for. All day long I would make calls to strangers that would either hang up or call me names. Or the several times a teenager answered the phone put on a terrible accent, and I became part of a sexual prank.

At the end of the day, which was around six, I tossed my headphones down, grabbed my knockoff Coach bag from Chinatown, and made my way to my crumbling studio apartment. I was single, no pets, no friends, no close family, and certainly no hot boyfriend I met while traveling the Caribbean islands. I sat in front of my small TV and chewed on whatever I could afford for the night, usually Taco Bell or McDonald's; my definition of a home-cooked meal was Ramen noodles.

At nine exactly I turned the television off, pulled an oversized Stetson University hoodie from an ex over my head, and sluggishly walked toward my double mattress, saying one day I'd get a bedframe. I would think at night, looking at the stars my ceiling windows revealed. I wouldn't be doing this much longer, going to a job I hated, being alone, purposeless. I had been assuring myself this for the last three years, only to repeat everything the next morning.

—◦◦◦—

This morning was all the same. I was going to be late for work, I looked an atrocity, and I hurriedly climbed down the black metal staircase, looking back to see my Italian landlord shaking his fist and yelling angry words that the construction workers' tools muffled. I hoped work to last forever, just to prolong the lecture I would have to hear from that man and another Oscar-worthy scene of me begging and promising to have all that I owe next month. I brought false tears to my eyes and a droopy shaken lip as I lied to my landlord, as if it were even a possibility my job would somehow produce the money I owed in one day. He knew I was lying. I knew I was lying. Every good tenant that paid on time knew I was lying.

I finally reached the thirteenth floor of my building and ran to my desk, trying to avoid the huge glass window my step-aunt Ester sat behind, which overlooked the whole office. I turned my laptop on, pulled up my call list, and as I lifted the outdated corded phone, I heard my aunt's black stiletto heels walking toward my desk. I panicked as everyone else did; all pretending they were on the phone with a potential client, which in this business did not exist.

My step-aunt gave me this job only because my Uncle Charlie had promised I'd be the hardest worker. With my uncle being ten years younger she just couldn't resist disappointing her boy toy. The first year I worked here I was the hardest worker. I had to be. I needed the money as a new New Yorker, and every other place I looked wasn't hiring. I worked double shifts, covered for anyone who needed the day off, and was always on time, even early. As the days grew into months and then another year, my admirable pace and loyalty faded, as I had the revelation that my paychecks were always the same distasteful number, and I wasn't being promoted.

My step-aunt stopped in front of my desk, her piercing, sunken-in, demonic-looking eyes caused a burning sensation on my head. I still persisted talking into the phone to no one and when the loud dial tone began, I quickly hung up and smiled to my step-aunt, who rolled her eyes and motioned her long, bony index finger to her office. I followed behind her. I could feel the vibration from her hard walk, as if she was breaking the marble floor apart and my clumsy steps were jumping over the debris.

All my co-workers put their phones back in the holsters as she passed and gravely looked at me, everyone knew nine times out of ten anyone who went into her office was fired. I had only been in her office once, the day I was hired. As she asked me to shut the door, I noticed the blue paint had faded since my first encounter with the devil. I sat in the leafed fabric chair in front of her wooden desk. There were four pictures of her and my uncle on their honeymoon in swimsuits, her long tongue in his mouth in every one; I shivered at them. Her office was nice, island themed. I admired a great interior design, which my apartment lacked.

My step-aunt had a stern look on her face, causing the wrinkles this month's Botox injection neglected to push forward, making her fifty-five look seventy. As she spoke about my daily tardiness and not meeting my weekly criteria, I imagined her as a preying mantis perched behind the desk. At any moment she could jump across and bite my head off.

When I zoned back into reality, she said, "Meaghan, I can't have you working here any longer. If I continue to let you come in late and not meet the standards I have set for everyone, my facility will be in a chaotic uproar. I cannot have a riot on my hands. This is a business. Meaghan, darling, you are family. That's the only reason I hired you in the first place." She placed her liver-spotted hands on her chest as if her heart ached. "Meaghan, I can't give you special privileges and allow you to do whatever you wish." Her voice all of a sudden went from caring and soft to low and dark.

"You're fired."

I couldn't even fathom the right words to say to her, so I left her in her office with her hands pushed together and a smirk on her face. I walked to my cubby, grabbed my purse and laptop, and headed for the elevator.

When I reached the outside, I felt nothing. I just got fired from a job I already despised, but I couldn't celebrate now that I was unemployed. I walked to the nearest bank and cashed my small 7.25 per hour check then ventured to Gino's café, treating myself to the rare lunch and coffee. I pushed my hands deep into my black pea coat pockets—the right one had a large hole—to avoid the cold spring air.

Coming upon my apartment building, I turned to take the back way and bumped into my land-lord, who had his chubby fingers on my escape black metal staircase. This confrontation was the last thing I wanted today.

"I took the liberty of pulling this back down for you. I've noticed you like using this and crawling through your window rather than taking the front door." His snotty smile disappeared, his face got red and when he lifted his hand. I knew this was not going to go smooth at all.

"Meaghan, don't you say one word. I let the last three months slide, trying to help you out, trusting that you'd pay me. Well it's the second, and you know what was due yesterday, Meaghan."

I opened my mouth to speak, but he continued. "This months' rent was due, and you know who I didn't receive this month's rent from?"

I opened my mouth again but he continued.

"You, Meaghan. I didn't get anything from you. Not last month's or the two before last. You know what this means?"

I didn't bother opening my mouth this time.

"It means you owe me four months now!"

I tried to intervene, but he just didn't stop.

"Here I am with all the rent from all my tenants but one, and I didn't even have to figure out whose was missing! Meaghan, I don't want to hear any more stories, no more tears, no more nothing. You're beyond past due, and I can't afford to have you stay here anymore,"

My eyes widened as I tried to speak.

"This is a business. If I keep letting you get away with not paying me, treating you special, I'll have a riot on my hands."

I felt as if I were having déjà vu.

"I don't even want the money anymore, Meaghan. You have until Friday to move out."

"But—"

"No buts, no nothing! Friday!"

I went to follow him, plead for mercy, but it was no use. He waved his hands and yelled "Friday!" two more times.

I took the black metal staircase and slipped through my paint-chipped window again with a warm tear sliding down my cold face. I shut my window and threw my bag on the orange, worn sofa, which I remember finding deserted in the hallway one summer and sliding it into my apartment. I sat on my double mattress and felt as if I were in some kind of purgatory, wandering purposeless with no job, no home, and realizing I'd have to call my mother and ask to stay with her, hearing her high-pitched squeal yelling to my father how thrilled and excited she is and only hearing my father's groans.

My younger brother, who was seventeen, would be down tomorrow to help move all my stuff to my parents' place, and I would be sleeping in my old room in the basement. My father's dreams of turning it into a pool hall would be crushed again upon my arrival. I went to the cardboard dumpster for some leftover boxes and began packaging the items worth salvaging. Later that evening, I looked at the clock, which read 6:15, and chuckled. I'd just be getting home from work. I jumped to look in my cabinets, opening and shutting them twice as if something delicious would appear. My hardest decision tonight was beef, chicken, or shrimp.

———

This morning was unlike any other morning. I woke up on my sofa to the noise of someone pounding on my door as opposed to my alarm. I pulled my sleeper's mask up and rubbed my tired eyes, yelling "Hold on!" in response to the constant knocks.

My little brother was not so little anymore; he stood overlooking me, tall like our father, his green eyes soft like our mothers. He wasn't scrawny anymore but toned, his jawline tight and sculpted like a GAP model.

"Bry, you grew," I said, reaching out for a hug, and to my surprise seeing a beautiful blonde girl, tanned, wearing pink lip-gloss and knee-high black leather heel boots.

Bryan hugged me tight and followed me in, holding the mystery girls' hand. He began the introductions as

I awkwardly stood unfashionably in my long johns and stained oversized hoodie.

"Meg, this is Cassie. She's my girlfriend. She came down to help, and you've never met, so yeah. What do you have to move?"

Cassie just stood there smiling like the sweetest little angel, and I was wiping this morning's drool from the corner of my mouth. She went to the bathroom. I told her she would have to wait one minute then flush. I congratulated my brother on having a beautiful girl. I changed my clothes and thought how the hell my brother was making moves while I was going backward. I walked into my living room to see them making out, and awkwardly, in envy, my eyes teared up.

Bryan, Cassie, and I, after twenty minutes of going from my apartment to my fathers' white moving van, were on our way to Franklin, Maine. Like a child leaving their favorite park, I looked back at the brick apartment building with a hope to return. I fell asleep on the drive, my head thumping against the window finally hard enough to wake me up and give a minor concussion as we pulled into my parents' driveway. Compared to all the homes in this small town, my parents had a big home, courtesy of my fathers' hardworking moving business and his cabinetry store, and my mothers' antique store, all in the center of town. It wasn't hard to own your own shop. Franklin was such a small town almost every family owned a small shop, all of us just living off of one another's needs.

My mother was standing at the front door, her hands clapped together, jumping up and down, screaming for my father. "They're here, George! They're here!"

To my surprise Cassie ran to my mother and hugged her, and then I walked up the steps in shock and hugged her. Cassie and my brother ran upstairs to his bedroom.

I stood in the foyer staring at my father until he said, "The basement's cold now, but in a few hours the heat will circulate enough to keep you warm through the night."

I shook my head up and down as my father moved out of the huddle and back onto his leather chair to watch the hunting channel, asking my mother when dinner would be finished. Nothing had changed about this place. The mediocrity set in quickly, reminding me why I had left in the first place.

I had a second, third, and fourth plate of my Mom's good food. She encouraged me all night to eat more, and I didn't hesitate; this was the first good meal I'd had in a while. After dinner I found my offered help in the kitchen wasn't needed as Cassie took the liberty of assisting my mother in my absence over the past year. I moseyed to the basement and pulled out the pullout couch. My father came out of the back room and gave me a set of sheets and my old Hello Kitty comforter. He touched the covered pool table as a last murmur to his dream.

I smiled and hugged him goodnight. When I heard the door shut, I grabbed my pillows, turned on the television, and began sobbing. I felt terrible. My brother would be moving out for college with his faithful girlfriend in the fall, and here I was, the older sibling, coming back to the very small town I had sworn I wouldn't miss.

I slept in longer that day than I had since my summers in high school. I awoke to my mother saying I had a visitor at the door. My first reaction was it was Mr. and Mrs. Applebum who lived next door to my family for as long as I could remember and brought all kinds of sweet things over every holiday, birthday party, or any occasion Mrs. Applebum desired to make a dessert. I climbed up the staircase and into the kitchen, routinely pulling my hair up on the way. When I reached the front door, no one was there. I opened the screen door to search, but the porch and the driveway were empty. Out of my peripheral, I saw a piece of paper that must have been ripped from a notebook; it was tucked into the underbelly of the mailbox. In black ink it read "Meaghan Groves." I quickly reached for the note. It had been folded four times, like a note you would pass to your crush in class.

> My dearest Meaghan,
>
> I expect you do not know of me nor have you ever seen or heard of me, but I assure you that I know you. Please do not be frightened. This is no ransom note or a threatening letter, merely a message of intrigue. When you were in high school you were the youngest person to work for the Franklin Weekly Paper. I never was a faithful reader, but when you wrote a dedication piece for you grandmother and her battle with breast cancer, I was deeply moved. I was hoping you would give me the honor of a visit to chat about the article. When I heard you were back in town, as you know all news travels fast

here, I was very excited and determined to meet you. I will list my address below. If you are free tomorrow, I would be very happy to see you at two o'clock.

Respectfully,
An admirer

Chapter 2

I read the note to no one. My family would have been totally against me visiting a stranger. I, however, was too curious and bored to give up on such an interesting adventure. I rummaged through my old boxes that night, searching for all my old newspaper articles. When I was in high school, the local paper needed an editor. I had good grammar skills and was going to be a graduate soon with the dream of being a journalist. That's all the paper owner needed to hear to put me on the job. Eventually he allowed me to write columns here and there about minute events in town, nothing too interesting, but the glimmer in my eyes when a journalist would bail and he would call me into his office to hand the assignment down was priceless.

The thought and hope of being a journalist was the motivation for me to move to New York. When I got there opportunity did not just magically appear how I pictured it would. My dreams of being a writer were pushed to the sidelines; the only thing I focused on was paying bills. I found the article I wrote in October. It was breast cancer awareness month, and my grandmother had recently lost her battle when I wrote it. All this time passed, and to receive a note from someone who remembered this small column was highly intriguing. I hardly slept all night long; this was the first time I can remember anticipating morning.

I rolled over to my mother's cat Lily sitting on the edge of the couch just staring at me. I pushed her aside to grab for my phone, which read 12:15. I jumped into the shower and had time to use the makeup basics I did understand. This had been the first time in years I'd taken the initiative to get ready and look presentable. I slipped on my black pea coat, and as quietly as possible, went upstairs, hoping no one would see me and question my whereabouts.

My mother's slim body was facing the steaming coffee pot. Her floral dress touched the floor, and the halter straps lifted everything, making her look a sight for sore eyes. I could see why my father fell in love with her; her beauty was timeless. I shut the door lightly, but my mother still heard.

She turned abruptly, startled. "Oh, Meaghan, I didn't know you were up yet. I know you've been catching up on your rest. Are you wearing makeup?" My mother's face looked surprised. I was also surprised. I hadn't had the care to pamper myself for some time, and I felt I looked good today, better than most days.

"Yeah, Mom. I'm going out for a while to catch up on some sights. Could I borrow the jeep?"

My mother tossed me her keys to the blue Grand Cherokee, "come by the shop later, and help with some new inventory," I hurried to the car, keeping a close eye on my watch and thinking up a scheme to get out of that conversation later.

I was very familiar with the streets of Franklin. The town was small enough to turn a corner and drive straight back into the center of town. I found my admirer's home fairly quickly and took no time to get out of the car and make my way to the white front door. The house was nice, brick like most, and had the evidence of a beautiful garden come summer. The quaint yard was protected by a black wooden fence.

I knocked once and heard heavy footsteps like boots. To my surprise a tall, handsome gentleman stood before me. He had hazel eyes that were soft, unlike his intimidating build. His thick brows gave a stern look, which disappeared when he smiled.

"How can I help you?"

"I got this note," I said, hesitantly pulling it from my left pocket and checking the address, unsure.

"This is my mom's writing." He looked perplexed and invited me in. "I'm not sure what all this is about, but she said she's been expecting you, and I've got to get to work." He put out his hand, and I shook it. "It was a pleasure meeting you…"

I shouted my name in nervousness, and he walked out of a back door in the kitchen. I sat there on a metal and fabric chair in the kitchen, yelling at myself silently for that class A response. I looked around, taking everything in—the tall stainless steel fridge, the old sepia-colored pictures hanging by bright floral magnets, the beautiful gray tiled floor, and the bright blue paint, which made me twist my face in distaste, remembering my boss' office.

I heard a creaking from the stairs, and in moments I was greeted by a smiling, middle-aged woman, who I presumed was my admirer. I stood, and she quickly and gently signaled me to sit.

"Can I get you anything to drink, darling?" She walked toward the coffee pot, and I accepted a strong cup of black coffee. Her movements were stiff, like she was in pain; her smile suggested otherwise. It was an exact replica of her son's. She stood around my mother's height, five foot six, I would guess. She was slender and had shoulder-length light brown hair. Her eyes were bright blue; I assumed her son got his from his father.

She sat down across from me, slow to reach her chair, and when she did she let out a long sigh of relief. "Well, you certainly look like your mother. I love her little jewelry store." She stirred her coffee with hazelnut creamer. "I was wondering, do you still write?"

I sipped my coffee and answered, one eyebrow raised. "I haven't for a while."

"Oh, what a shame. I think you have a real talent. I was going through old papers last week and saw your column peeking out of one of my files. I reread it, and it moved me more than the first time I read it." She looked at me as if she were about to suggest something.

"I appreciate that. It was an article close to heart for me and my family. It was such a small thing, though, really just for the Franklin paper, ma'am, nothing like the New Yorker." I sipped my coffee again. The brisk air from the crooked window above the sink began to cool my coffee rapidly.

My admirer, who introduced herself as Georgia Harvest and nothing more, noticed me shiver and pulled the window tighter. "Old house," she murmured, sitting down in agony again then smiling reassuringly. "I really had hoped you were still a writer. You see, I have a story that I would like to share with my small family, my story. A sort of memoir for when I'm not around."

I just sat there puzzled. This woman wanted me to write a memoir of her? I just met her, and I was no grand author. "Georgia, I'm incredibly honored that you would ask me to do this project, but why? I mean, I just can't. This is such a big thing. Why don't you write it?"

Georgia chuckled. "I'm no writer, dear. That's why I've asked you, and I'll compensate you for your time. Surely you could do this?"

I sipped my coffee once more and stood. "Thank you for this incredible offer, but I haven't written in some time, and I just don't think I can do this."

She showed me to the front door, still smiling, and told me to please reconsider. I pulled out of her rocky driveway, heading for my mother's store.

"You're awfully quiet, Meaghan," my mother said, handing a lady her small bag filled with costume pearls.

I plopped up on the counter and explained to my mother the events that took place today.

"Well, why don't you do it? That's an incredible opportunity, and didn't you want to be a writer? Now, see, you have a job offer your first day back, and you moved away from me for three years with no such luck. It's a sign, honey. Take it."

I knew my mom was right; this had been what I was searching for, a purpose.

—❧—

I went to Georgia's home the next morning, eager and nervous to begin a story I had no idea would change my life completely. We again went to the kitchen. This time I offered her a chair and insisted on me getting drinks and such, since I would be a guest every day. I wouldn't work under such conditions of her straining herself. With much disagreement, I finally got Georgia to sit down and let out her sigh of relief.

Her son, Noah, the handsome gentleman who greeted me on my first arrival, came into the kitchen with a large blue tote, sat it in the middle of the table, and said his good-byes, kissing his mother on the forehead and waving me farewell.

"What's this?" I asked, running my fingers over the lid.

"It's the beginning to the end," Georgia responded, smiling, gesturing me to pop off the lid and take a look.

Inside there had to be hundreds or thousands of pictures—some old and worn, their tattered corners revealing their age, others new digital-quality photos, one I noticed of Noah and Georgia taken yesterday.

"One of the terms I must set if you are going to do this project, Meaghan, is you much accept my challenge." She became very serious and looked me in the eye, a sort of look that made me take a seat and made my ears perk up like those of a terrier.

"Your challenge?" I questioned, placing both hands together on the cold wooden table centered with a bowl of plastic fruit.

"My son Noah agreed to it earlier this year, and I have asked others to do it as well. Every day for one year you have to take a picture of anything—you, your family, your garden, strangers, anything!" She was in an excited uproar now. "Everyday, no exceptions!"

"Why?" I asked, intrigued.

Georgia pursed her lips and gently said, "A gentleman once told me, 'Georgia, you've got to fully embrace life,' and I thought over the years how better to embrace life than by capturing every day? The only way I know how to do that is take a picture. So are you up for that challenge?" Georgia's anxious eyes looked at me.

I'd never heard of such a challenge, but I agreed and informed her I would do my best to keep up with it.

"Oh hush, child, all you've got is time. Promise me you'll do it. Promise you'll capture every moment."

And I did. I pulled out my cellphone and took my first picture. It was of Georgia beside her tote of memories.

I pushed my phone back into my old messenger bag, the very one I used to use back in high school when I worked for the paper. "Are there any other terms I should know about before we begin?" I asked, smiling at Georgia. Her quirkiness and kindness were the contagious type; she made me smile for no reason.

"Yes, there is one more term, Meaghan, and it is very important to me that this project stay between you and me only." She looked out the back window and then out the front. "I asked you here to write a memoir for my family, and when I say family, I mean my son. I was diagnosed with breast cancer."

My movements froze; I already had a hint to where this was going.

"I am a grateful woman, Meaghan. I have seen a lot, loved a lot, and embraced my life. I refuse to go through chemo and have my son cater to my every handicap need, causing him to miss out on life. That's what the challenge is all about. That's why I make it a necessary measurement, and by all means, you cannot tell Noah. I will inform him when the time is right."

I said nothing. My muscles were tensed, my mouth dry, and she just sat there tapping the side of her Martha Stewart coffee mug, waiting for my response. I wasn't sure how to view this woman anymore, a sweet lady or a total basket case.

"Well, say something. I'm having hot flashes over here!" Georgia smiled and waved her hand as if to fan herself.

"Georgia, I don't know if I can do this anymore. I mean, I can't do this. I just met you and your son, and to keep something like that from him… I just couldn't lie to anyone, and won't he start to wonder why I'm here every day? I mean, it's bound to get out." I searched her eyes for any change of mind.

"If you didn't say anything and I didn't say anything, it would never get out, and I don't want to ruffle your feathers, but I'm the one dying over here. You're just the writer." She smiled and spoke sarcastically as if to simmer the mood. Georgia's hand fell on top of mine as she continued, "Meaghan, please, I need this to be done so I can have a peace of mind, so Noah can look back and read all about me when I'm not here. You are a great writer. If you could conjure up something half as wonderful as what you wrote for your grandmother and your family, I would be entirely grateful."

I still looked up at her worriedly.

"And if you don't want to do it for me, at least do it for the money. I'm sure you haven't found a job already, and everyone could use money. Come on, what do you say?"

I sat and thought. I did need the money to get back into my own place, and the faster I could, the better, but I didn't think I would be able to keep such a secret, especially if Noah began to question things. The constant stare and warm smile across the table convinced me to utter yes, and with that Georgia clapped and laughed.

"Well it's late now. Noah will be home soon. I only want to work on it when he's at work, so I'll see you tomorrow, hun!"

I left Georgia's place with a feeling I can only describe as when I've drink milk a day past its best by date, the unsure feeling it settles in my stomach, the debate whether I'll be all right or it'll cause chaos.

I sat in my basement petting Lily, who sat on top of the black printer. As soon as it started printing my picture of Georgia, she jumped on to the floor and bolted up the stairs. The glossy paper the photo printed out on gave a glare to Georgia's white smile, making her appear friendlier and warm-hearted. I smiled and took an orange sharpie from the pencil holder my father once used to write pool scores down. I flipped the picture and wrote "Georgia Harvest Challenge: Day One."

Chapter 3

Each picture she lifted had an hour's worth of story. Some made her smile; others made her tear up. I was having so much fun the next few days hearing her stories of boys she dated, arguments she had, her siblings, and her schooling, our time just flew by. Every day I would wait until Noah left to come in and then leave ten minutes before he was due back. I felt so terrible at the end of our visits, like an unfaithful wife leaving and sneaking around to see someone else.

He had Sundays off, so I would stay home with my family and long for the next day. I became so encapsulated with Georgia's story—all her accomplishments, her journeys—and we had just started. Each night I would collect all my notes from the day.

When I would go long periods of time without my pen touching the paper, Georgia would say, "You writing anything down?" then smile as always.

I looked at my notes tonight and decided I had better start writing something before everything caught up to me. Georgia was born in Baton Rouge, Louisiana, before her mother moved somewhere up north. Her late mother's name was Ellis, and she never met her father, but her birth certificate read Wesley Harvest.

"My mother," she began, handing me two old pictures with a stunning brunette in a long dark dress and long hair who looked just like Georgia, "she was such a hardworking woman. She worked in a diner all day.

My older sister Marlene would take care of me and my older brother until our mother got home late at night just in time to see us to bed and tell us she loved us."

Georgia shook her head. "She really worked herself to death. She died at the age of forty-five." Georgia wiped a tear from her slightly wrinkled face. "She had to go through the unfortunate event of being a mother who buried her child first, my sister Marlene. She wed when she was twenty-two and died of an automobile accident with her bridegroom. She was so young and beautiful."

Georgia passed me a picture of three children and pointed to the tallest, Marlene. "An old drunkard driving a newspaper truck hit their vehicle, pushing them through a stop sign, and traffic killed the two of them who would have otherwise survived the first hit."

I looked closely at my watch, always paranoid to keep track of time.

"That really devastated all of us, but especially my mother. My brother was now a teenager and looked after me after his paper route in the morning. My mother continued to work at the diner, opening and closing, always making the effort to come and give us all the affection we needed at night. She was a good woman." Georgia's eyes were filled to the rim with tears, as were mine.

When I arrived home I hugged everyone in my family, even Cassie. It's an interesting thing that the thought of losing a loved one makes you appreciate them completely. Everyone thought something was wrong because of how tightly I hugged them, but one thing I learned from Georgia Harvest was to appreciate everything, because nothing's a given, and especially appreciate family. I snapped a picture of everyone in the living room. The back read, "Georgia Harvest Challenge: Day Four.

———✍———

We would pick back up where we left off, always at her home. I offered to take us to lunch or for coffee often, but Georgia feared Noah would see us and ask too many questions. And she enjoyed the simpler things, saying to me, "Why would I pay for a cup of coffee with a fancy label when I've got grounds, filters, and a pot right here?"

That settled it; we ate turkey sandwiches and drank coffee today while she continued with her childhood.

"My brother Elton, like most boys, was girl crazed." She laughed at the thought. "He would get me from school in our mother's car, drop me off, speed through my homework, often doing it for me, put cartoons on the tube, and fly out of the house, making me promise if our mother ever asked he was here the whole time. In reality he would leave and pick up girls in the car. He was mighty popular, saying it was his car. Most high school boys then didn't have their own. In the evenings he would run in the house, fix me something to eat, and drive to the diner in the nick of time to get my mother from work."

I laughed, thinking of the schemes my brother must have conjured up for my father to allow him to take the jeep out at nights.

"Where's Elton now?" I asked, like a kid on the edge of their seat during a scary movie, their eyes skimming the screen for the monster's next position.

Georgia sighed. "When our mother died, I had just started working at the very diner she gave her soul to. I was living in the same house with Elton and his fiancé Leina, the girl he would often pick up during high school." She sipped her hot coffee, not forgetting to blow on it first.

"We worked together to pay the bills, and everything was honky dory, but I stood there one day in the diner, serving the very same cheesecake my mother had served for years. I heard everything in that moment, everyone speeding past me, the cars, the bell on the door swinging back and forth as one customer after the next piled in, the hairy cook my mother often complained at nights about his smell yelling orders, and the register drawer slamming shut while the old waitress who wore entirely too much makeup chewed pink bubblegum.

"In that moment I threw my polka-dotted apron on to the sticky checkered tile, took my tips, and quit. When my brother heard, he was furious. He told me to walk back there and get my job back. I said no, that I wasn't going to be like our poor mother, working all day and night, for what? I had no children to take care of, I was young, and I wanted to see the world—not even the world, just something different. My brother thought I was being ridiculous. He was fine with the same house, the same people, the same everything. He grabbed his gray sport's jacket and his keys and told me c'mon, that we were going to get my job back. I stood there with tears running down my face and said, 'No, I refuse to slave like mother.' Elton came storming across the room and slapped me." Georgia rubbed the side of her cheek. "I had enough money saved up to get a start on my traveling by myself, so I packed a large green suitcase and hit the bus. That was the last time I saw Elton."

I sat in awe, collecting everything I had heard. Georgia looked at the wooden clock on the wall above me and said she'd see me tomorrow. I took a stop at the small coffee corner for something refreshing, a muffin perhaps. When I made it to the front of the line I heard a familiar voice behind me, and after quickly placing my order for a blackberry muffin, I locked eyes with Noah.

"Hey stranger." He smiled, making me blush; I instantly felt the heat on my cheeks.

"Hi, Noah. How are you?" I was holding the line up now.

The anxious cashier murmured, "Mm hmm!"

I stood aside. Noah asked for me to wait so he could walk me to my car. I quickly told him it was unnecessary; however, he persisted. The nosy cashier handed him his coffee and an apple strudel churro, which he insisted were Georgia's favorite. I quickly figured him for the kind of Prince Charming I dreamed about as a little girl. He was handsome, generous, and loving, very much like his mother.

I awkwardly followed beside him as we walked out of the café, and I listened to his talk about the weather picking up soon and many rainy spring days he predicted. Then he touched on the one subject I was praying to avoid.

"So why did my mom want to see you the other day? I mean, how do you know her?" His eyes twinkled with innocence.

I felt terrible that I knew something he should know, and several times I wanted to just blurt it all out like a confession tape. "Oh I don't know her."

He looked puzzled.

"I mean I didn't know her." I inserted an hellish awkward laugh. "I used to write for the paper here in town, and your mother happened to be some type of a fan." I noticed I was flailing my arms and laughing the whole time I spoke. He must have thought I was ludacris. "She was kind enough to invite me over and speak with her about some of my articles."

I could tell his mind was calculating all types of things, so I quickly walked to my car and told him it was nice seeing him. As I pulled away he waved. In the mirror I saw him looking my way, his hands in his pockets.

—☙☙—

Georgia Harvest Challenge: Day Five was a sort of Andy Warhol picture of Campbell's Chicken Noodle soup. The cold spring air between New York and here gave me some kind of sickness. I called Georgia, who insisted I stay in bed and drink hot tea with lots of honey, and I didn't hesitate to do exactly that.

Throughout my hours of sleeping I would wake up for moments at a time. Twice I saw Lily just staring at me. Once my mother was shaking me and telling me I had a visitor in the kitchen.

"It's a boy!" she yelled.

I raised my head to say "What?" but my mother was already running back up the stairs.

I heard her say, "She'll be right up."

I panicked. I jumped out of bed. I was wearing a long baseball tee and sweats, my hair was sticking to my sweating face, and I had tissues falling from my pockets. My mother called for me.

"Coming!" I squeaked, my voice still altered from my cough.

I pulled my hair back and shook my head in the mirror, giving up all hope and making my way up the steps. I saw Noah standing by our dining room table, my father laughing while putting his hand on Noah's shoulder. I hadn't seen my father laugh like that in some time. My mother came swooping behind them, offering sun tea or coffee. Noah took the tea and looked up at me.

I put my hands in my sweats and asked if I was interrupting. My father nodded and went to sit in front of the TV. My mother stood in between Noah and I, just smiling, until I said, "Mom, do you mind?"

She said, "Oh, of course not. He's here to see you." She hustled back to the kitchen.

I invited Noah to the porch. He held a small brown cardboard box in his hands.

"What's that?" I asked.

"Oh I hit a small animal on the way here. I boxed it up, thinking you would want it." Noah smiled.

"Oh really." I laughed then coughed, suddenly losing my breath.

"Ouch, that sounds like rough stuff. My mom heard you were having a cold. She asked me to bring this over to you. It's some tea bags, honey and two turkey sand-wiches. She also told me you'd be coming over often, hanging out with her, I believe were her exact words." Noah handed me the box.

I was stunned Georgia told him I would be around. "Let me ask you something. Aren't you young to be hanging out with my mom all day?"

I mustered up a conclusion faster than I could ever remember. "Nonsense, she is a sweet woman who admires a good write and conversation. I just so happen to admire the same." I looked at Noah to see if he was buying it. He smiled, watching me walk to the bench my mother had my father tote home from the curbside some years back.

"She inspires me to write more, something I lost sight of." I had come to the realization Georgia had me doing something I was always yearning for. "You're not trying to crush my dreams are you, Noah?" I smiled and then thought, God, Meaghan, are you flirting?

"Certainly not, I just want to make sure my mother's in good hands." Noah started to walk off the porch.

"Well, I certainly won't be boxing up any dead ani-mals and bringing them to her, if that's what you mean," I said, smiling and thanking him for my care package.

He waved bye, flashing his contagious smile as he backed out of the driveway. I took a deep breath before I was flooded with questions. My mother was stand-ing by the door, my father was still watching TV, and my brother was on the bottom step, making smooching faces like a little kid.

"No, he's not my boyfriend. Yes, I do think he is handsome. No, we are not having sexual relations. This is a care package from his mother who, yes, I am friends with, and, no, he did not kiss me good-bye."

No one said anything, and I walked back to the basement and treated myself to a Georgia Harvest turkey sandwich before falling back to sleep, dreaming of Georgia getting on a bus and embarking on our journey.

Chapter 4

It was one week before I was able to see Georgia. I was diagnosed with a common cold, and Noah stopped by twice more with care packages. I continued to take my pictures, though, as Georgia inquired in a note taped to the plastic wrap on my turkey sandwich. My pictures were terribly dull: one of Lily, who jumped at the slightest movement, and one of my mother washing dishes. A good one of Cassie and my brother, who actually took the liberty to frame it, and the others of tissues and medicine, blooming plants, and such. I was so very happy when I finally felt well enough to walk out of the house and breathe fresh air. While I had been inside, trees were budding, the green grass was peeking through the topsoil, and more and more people were coming out of their homes with garbage bags, beginning spring cleaning.

My first stop this morning was the coffee shop. I had decided to pick up a dozen apple strudel churros to thank Georgia for her kindness. This was the first time I pulled into her driveway and got out of my car while Noah was there. It felt almost perfect.

"Hey!" he said, making his way to his truck and looking at the white box in my hand.

"No, it's not a dead animal," I said, laughing.

"Oh, you look much better. I see my mom's remedies suited you well." Noah grabbed my messenger bag and slipped it back on to my shoulder.

"Yeah, they definitely helped, thanks."

Noah could tell I felt uncomfortable that close to him, and like a gentleman, backed away, saying his farewell, and he was off to work. I watched him pull away. Flicking the loose hair out of my face and looking up, I saw Georgia standing by the door, smiling. When I got closer, I noticed Georgia had lost some weight; she appeared frail and walked slower, more hesitantly than the last time.

"Hey, Georgia."

She hugged me like a mother hugs her daughter. "Hey, honey. Oh, you sound much better." She motioned toward the kitchen as usual.

"Yes, thanks to you and Noah. You made me feel great. Oh, here." I grabbed for the bakery box. "They're apple strudel churros. I ran into Noah at the café before I got sick, and he told me they were your favorite."

She hugged me once more, telling me she had her first when she was in New Mexico. She said ever since then they'd been a sweet addiction. I showed her some of the pictures I had been taking. She fell for Lily instantly, comparing her to a cat she once had named Baby while she lived with an Aunt Loretta in Nevada. She said the budding of the trees reminded her of when she passed through New Jersey, the garden state. After hearing all this I decided we should pick back up where we left off.

"So," she began, pouring her hazelnut creamer into her coffee while stirring it with a silver spoon. "I got on the bus and then another and then one more, never paying attention to where they were heading. When I got off the last bus, I decided I had better call a friend of my mother's. Her name was Elena, and my mother had kept in touch with her for some time, and then I hadn't heard her mention her name ever again. I had remembered meeting her twice, and she said if us kids ever needed anything to call her, so I took full advantage of that statement."

Georgia recalled pulling her mother's contact book from her bag and flipping through to find Elena. When she did she connected right through.

"Hello, Elena, this is Georgia, Georgia Ellis's daughter. Yes, it was very tragic. I have a favor to ask. Do you still live in Mississippi? New Mexico? Well, could I stay with you for a little while? Yes, everything's fine. I'm just exploring. Great, I'll see you soon then!"

Georgia smiled. "I was so excited to be going somewhere and doing something. I got on a few more buses, and when I made it to New Mexico, I had my first hitchhiking experience."

Georgia took a bite of her churro and offered me one. I accepted, feeling like I was in New Mexico with her. I pressed her to please continue.

"Well, I got to New Mexico, and it was hot, very hot. I felt after I got off the bus I would faint. I walked for some time, thinking it would not be a far walk to Elena's home, but every step killed me. I was dripping sweat and had to just sit down. I wiped my forehead and sat up against a worn gas station. I wandered inside for a cold drink, getting water and cola. When I went back outside, there was a blue car being pumped by a service man and a slender woman with two young boys sitting in the back seat. She gave them each change and told them to hurry back. With that they ran into the store, frantically searching through all the packets of candy. The woman whose name I would learn was Candice pulled her brown glasses down, revealing her sparkling green eyes. She was a beautiful woman. Her face was porcelain like a doll's, except for the dark purple circle around her right eye, and as she pushed her glasses back up, I noticed her top lip was swollen also.

"Her two boys, who she called Tyler and Tobias, spoke with her for a moment then unexpectedly ran over to me, saying, 'Our mother would like us to ask you if you want a ride.' They hit each other, trying to speak at the same time, and smiled, revealing missing teeth and all their freckles bunched up. I looked up at the woman, who smiled and beeped her horn with her white leather gloves. The two boys picked up my suitcase and lifted it in to the back seat with all their might, and Tobias opened the door for me.

"'Hello there, Ms…?'

"'Georgia, Georgia Harvest.'

"Georgia shook my hand like she had Candice's. 'Georgia Harvest, so where you heading?'

"I showed her the address. She told me it would be about forty-five minutes and to get comfortable. She also asked me if I ever took a drive from a stranger before. I told her no and gave her a short summary of how I got here. She said she understood perfectly well and began to tell me hers.

"'I worked at a diner too. It's my husband's, though. He put me to work mornings and then gave me money to do whatever the rest of the day.' She pulled a tiny cigar from a velvet case and had me light it for her. 'I quickly found out that—' She stopped speaking and told her boys to cover their ears. 'I found out that I worked mornings, because all evening he would flirt with the younger waitresses. He started taking them out to dinner and even made the mistake to bring one home, and—' She turned to make sure the boys' ears were covered. 'And did his deed with her.'

"I gasped at the thought. 'What did you do?'

"Georgia leaned forward, reenacting what she had done to Candice. 'I packed up what I needed and told the boys to go wait in the car while I got everything together. When I got to the door, my husband stood there with an ugly grin on his face and asked me where I was going.' She tapped her cigar as we stopped at an intersection. 'Long story short, I got out of there as fast as I could, but not before he branded me.' She sat, looking straight into my eyes. The dark circle intensified the look in her green eyes, pulling out a small black bag with rolls of cash peeking through. 'And not before I cleared out our joint account.' She smiled and told the boys they could uncover their ears now as she stepped on the gas, pulling forward.

"We all laughed and cheered ourselves to Candice's toast of 'the hell with men, here's to making our own!' I slept the rest of the drive.

"Candice shook me while the sun was setting and whispered, 'You're here.'

"I wanted to wake the boys and say thank you, but Candice insisted I didn't. She said they hated good-byes. I hugged Candice and wished her and the boys the best of luck. She pulled out fast, hitting the highway, and I made my way to Elena Marshall's front steps.

"Elena showed me straight to her kitchen, satisfying my long hunger with a hearty pot of roast and beans and plenty of sweets, including a peculiar dessert called a churro afterward. She kept saying how much I looked like my mother, reminiscing on my mother and her old charades. I enjoyed hearing stories about my mother when she was younger and more energetic.

"I fell asleep quickly that night. The heat had done a number on me. In fact, when I awoke the next morning my shoulders were sunburnt."

Georgia touched her the tops of her shoulders as if she could still feel the burn.

"Elena told me her husband was on a fishing trip. I hadn't known she was married, but she assured me he wouldn't be back for another two weeks and that by then she would hope I was on my way. Elena marveled at my story so far, saying that I was adventurous and wild like my mother was. She laughed at the thought of the two of them back in the day. Elena had several photos of my mother and her standing with school books, or in long chic dresses when my mother was crowned prom queen, standing with a tall, handsome gentleman that almost reminded me of my brother Elton."

Georgia stood for more coffee, but I managed to get her to stay seated and continue while I started a fresh pot.

"That evening I got to drive Elena's truck through the long dirt field out back. I laid on top of the hood, staring at the bright stars shining through the dark night sky. I thought about my brother and what he might be doing now, probably still complaining about my immature moves and how he was expecting me to walk back in any moment. I laughed at the very thought of it all. I wished he would see the good in it all one day. I had a whole map of opportunity and dreams at my fingertips."

Georgia looked over at the pot, which just finished dripping. It was my signal to pour her a cup. She nodded her head in thanks and continued.

"I could see after a few days why my mother had liked Elena so much. She was very intelligent, very funny, and just as sweet as honey. When it rolled around to the second week, Elena got to be very nervous, asking me when I'd be leaving and where I would be off too. She put money in my pocket to help pay for the way. I figured she hadn't told her husband I was staying, and for whatever reason that was a problem. I had called my Aunt Loretta in Nevada, who was the only sibling my mother ever spoke about her having. I hadn't talked to her in years, but my mother spoke to her often right up until her death. Aunt Loretta was happy to have me stay and had a small antique shop her and her husband owned that I could work at for as long as my stay.

"The next night I was awaken by Elena, who was in a fiery rant with herself in the kitchen. I came out as quickly as possible, stopping at the corner.

"She was walking back and forth, sweating. 'Wes will have my head for sure if he comes home to her.' Elena was fidgeting now and looked up at me, her eyes crazed like a mad woman. 'Oh Georgia, my sweet Georgia peach, you understand, don't you?' She came toward me, grabbing my shoulders and sobbing now. 'Your mother was so beautiful. She could have had any man she wanted, any man she wanted!'

"Elena walked back to the kitchen sink. I took note of a now empty bottle of scotch on the counter. 'She just had to have my Wesley, my Wesley.' Elena held up the black-and-white picture of my mother in her prom gown kissing the tall, handsome man. Elena was in the far back corner just staring at my mother. 'I was in love with him. I would have done anything for him, but he fell for Ellis, like all the rest of them did.'

"I felt tears building up in my eyes now. My mind was slowly shifting the puzzle pieces together.

"'Georgia, I loved him, and he wanted her, only her. They moved in together and had children together, and I just sat there and watched her perfect family grow while I sat on the sideline.' Elena looked at me now, wild and sympathetic. 'You have to leave, Georgia. If Wesley knew, he'd kill me.'

"Tears were steadily streaming down my face now. 'Finish the story, Elena.'

"Elena fell to the ground, her face buried in her hands.

"'That's why my mother stopped speaking to you, isn't it? Isn't it!' I was yelling at that point.

"Elena raised her head and continued, 'Your mother was working. Wesley was injured and sitting at home unable to work. Your mother trusted me to stay with him while she was gone to watch Marlene and Elton and yourself. I fell in love with him even more, Georgia.

He wanted to leave and marry me. I knew it was wrong for him to leave his family, but I wanted him. He was always supposed to be mine.'

"I grabbed Elena's shoulders, shaking her like a rag doll, full of rage and hate. 'My mother trusted you! She trusted you! Do you know what she went through?' I screamed, and Elena sobbed, sitting there in a pile of shame and guilt.

"I stormed down the hall and grabbed my belongings. As I walked back out of the bedroom, I heard a man's deep voice.

"'What the hell is wrong, Elena?'"

"I froze at the sight of a tall man towering over Elena, who held his legs and stared at me, murmuring she was sorry, so sorry."

Georgia wiped a tear, which had made its way to her jawline. "That was the first time I ever saw my father. He looked just like Elton. My sister Marlene had had his nose, and I, I had his eyes." She looked up at the clock and suggested I get a head start home. She wanted to clean herself up before Noah got back, or he would know she was in shambles.

I wanted to keep going. I begged to know what happened next. Georgia smiled and said, "All in good time."

Georgia Harvest Challenge: Day Twelve was the starry night sky, which the camera couldn't capture the full beauty of. I took this photo outside of my parents' home. I closed my eyes and lay on the warm hood of the jeep, placing myself in New Mexico with Georgia. Her story was so incredible, full of action and such suspense. Every time we stopped I longed for her to continue.

I sat outside for about three hours that night, so many thoughts running through my head. Georgia looked so weak today. Noah probably hadn't noticed because he sees her every day, but I could tell she was much smaller. How much longer would she wait to tell him she was dying? How much longer before he hated me? I began looking forward to seeing him, stopping by the café more often just for us to bump into each other, waking up earlier and making time to pamper myself for any occasion I might see him. Noah was just in the neighborhood more often, coming by my mother's shop and helping my father with moving appointments since Cassie and my brother were going to more out-of-town raves. He was often invited to dinner by one of my parents, and we even became part of each other's picture challenge.

The first time we were inside of my mother's jewelry store, I had on ten rings and an old feather scarf. He laughed hysterically, telling me to hold that pose, and snap! I wanted nothing more than to spend time with him and Georgia. Georgia began starting her conversations by asking what Noah and I were up to. I found I was telling her more about our story than actually writing hers. She claimed Noah hadn't talked so much about a girl since Lucie Gale in the seventh grade. I laughed, looking at his school picture from that year with blocks of metal covering his wide smile.

I sat in Georgia's kitchen, the windows creaked open now that it was slightly warmer out, listening to "Do You Love Me" by the Contours, waiting for Georgia to say the sun tea was done. It was now my guilty craving during our conversations.

Georgia poured me a full glass and told me my kidneys were going to shrivel. Then she laughed and said, "But it's so good, isn't it?"

I shook my head yes while both of my hands were tightly wrapped around the striped glass cup, drinking in gulps.

"So where did we leave off?"

I flipped through my notes to prepare writing. I knew exactly where we left off. "You saw you're father and were leaving Elena's."

Georgia smiled. I felt she knew where she left off also but was always checking to see if she bored me. "Yes, so I walked out of Elena's home. The look my father had given me was like a deer-in-the-headlights look. He never dreamt he'd ever see me again, and when he did, he just stood there speechless. I turned and walked out of that place with my head held high, just walking into the dark early morning into an endless dirt plain. I never turned back around, but I felt his eyes on my back as I was walking.

"I reached a main road after about an hour of walking, saw headlights, and figured I would give hitchhiking another try. I stuck my hand up like I was calling a taxi. A young man, not much older than I at the time, pulled up in a green Cadillac.

"'Don't you know you're supposed to hold your thumb out, miss?' He had a wonderful smile.

"'Well, I'm new to this.' We both laughed.

"He asked me where I was headed, and I told him, "Nevada, but I'd go as far as you could take me.'

"He laughed and told me to hop in. 'Well, miss, you're in luck. I'm headed to Las Vegas. That'll be just about the whole trip for you.'

"We started off our journey and hit it off swell. His nickname was Flint. He said that's all he went by, and there was no use in calling him otherwise.

"'I got it when I was younger. I had a quick temper.'" He looked over to me and smiled. "'I can assure you I grew out of it, miss.'

"He drove and stopped here and there for small lunches and drinks. I learned he was headed to Las Vegas to be a musician on the strip with high hopes that some record label would stop by and sign a deal with him.

"'That's very ambitious,' I said as we spoke over lunch at a small truck stop diner. I had a turkey club; he had a grilled cheese and greasy fries.

"'No, I think what you're up to is very ambitious. Others would call it a death sentence. It just fires me up, Georgia. So many people think they're living when they can't fathom the half.'

"Flint was the most passionate person I had ever met. He was so determined to be a musician. I couldn't picture anything coming in between him and his drive, until I had a few encounters with Flint's temper.

"Flint was tired and had fallen asleep in the passenger seat. He had asked me to drive, saying he wasn't confident in his nighttime driving skills. I quickly took the opportunity to drive, as I had wanted to all this time. I was driving for about four hours when I decided to pull over. After drinking so much water, naturally I had to use the restroom. I stopped at a small gas station. When I went in Flint was steadily snoring. When I came out, he was in a fitted uproar.

"'Who the hell do you think you're dealing with? You think I'm a fool?' Flint was standing outside of the car with a crazed look in his eyes.

"I swore I didn't understand what he was talking about.

"He slapped the hood so hard I jumped. "I'm not dumb, Georgia.' He grabbed my arm hard and pulled me toward the car, alerting the gentleman in the gas station.

"'Flint, what are you talking about?'

"'My wallet was in that brown bag right there.' He pulled me closer. 'Right there!'

"I started crying. I had never been grabbed like that in my life. I was crying in fear. I didn't know what he would do next, and then I saw the corner of a brown wallet sticking out from underneath the seat.

"'There it is! There it is!' I said, pointing.

"Flint pulled it out and counted all the money in it. It was all there, of course. 'Sorry, Georgia,' he said, speaking as if nothing had happened. 'It must have fallen out and slid under the seat.' Flint looked at me for only a moment. I saw the mad look in his eyes slowly disappear, and in seconds the kind, soft-spoken Flint I had encountered earlier came back to the surface.

"'It's fine,' I said, still in shock and embarrassed. A few bystanders stood by their cars, gossiping amongst themselves.

"Flint walked into the gas station to use the restroom, and I sat in the car just waiting, thinking if

I should continue to take this trip with him, but it was just too much to risk. He was going straight through Nevada. If I didn't then I would have to hitchhike with different people, and there was a chance I wouldn't be picked up. Flint was walking back to the car. I decided to stay and take my chances. I was still very frightened of the event that had occurred, and I hardly talked the rest of the way, just making casual weather conversation to cover the miles."

Georgia sat stirring sugar into her tea. She raised her head slowly to watch the small raindrops turn to large ones, causing a flooding downpour in a matter of seconds. Looking in her eyes, I felt the weather began to coincide with her story.

For a moment we just sat in silence. She stirred her tea, never taking a sip, like this was the first time she had ever revisited the thought she was reliving every moment. She closed her eyes from time to time, transitioning from her past back to reality. One second she was looking at me; the next I'm sure Flint was across from her.

I laid my cheap ballpoint pen down on my yellow tablet paper and reached for a napkin to wipe the small puddle condensation on the table. Georgia remained practically motionless; my movements did not phase her. Her eyes continued straight down into her cup.

"Georgia?" I said. "Then what?" I urged to her to press on.

Georgia lifted her head and asked me if the room temperature was okay. I said yes and again questioned what happened next.

Georgia smiled. "I drove a little while longer. It was hotter as we journeyed. We stopped more often for water and rest. Flint was very kind the next day. We were sitting at a large gas station. The back part had a bar and was a small diner, and all sorts of pies filled the front case. We sat down and ordered small things, sandwiches, and Flint insisted on me trying Boston crème pie. He said it was his favorite. His mother was a Bostonian and entered in a baking contest annually. Her crème pie always took first place.

"I grabbed for my glass of water when Flint said my name, softer than he ever had before. 'Georgia.' He put his hand on the back of his neck, barely making eye contact with me.

"'Yes? What's wrong?' I questioned.

"'I wanted to apologize for yesterday. It's just I really thought you might be one of those women who go around country stealing from guys like myself, oblivious that a beautiful woman would ever do anything wrong.' Flint smirked and shook his head at the thought. 'I felt like an idiot for accusing you. You are just a beautiful woman. I never met to hurt you. Could you ever forgive me?'

"Flint looked so sincere. I could tell he really meant it, so of course I was quick to touch his shoulder and tell him, 'No hard feelings, Flint. I mean, we had a long day, and the afternoon was hotter than hell. The heat really gets to you, you know? And to be honest, if I heard stories like that, I would have thought the same thing. Maybe I would have reacted differently, but it's the past now.' I lifted up my glass of water, and he lifted his.

"'Here's to a smooth trip on a road to dreams, Georgia!'

"All day long it seemed time pasted so quickly. Things were no longer awkward, and we had a deeper connection, telling some of our childhood stories. I told him of Elton, and he told me of his father kicking him out at the thought of his child being a delusional rock star. Flint and I shared many laughs that day. By nightfall we entered into Nevada. We were so excited. I had stopped to call my Aunt Loretta and prepare her for my arrival, and she informed me she would pick me up in Las Vegas where Flint would be stopping. We decided to rest and make the short trip to Vegas in the morning so we'd be refreshed, and I'd get to explore the strip a little while before Flint and I departed.

"Flint pulled over in the middle of the plain just off the highway. The air was humid, and the stars were bright. I crawled into the back seat to lie down. I fell asleep quickly. My eyes were tired from the heat. To my surprise, when I rolled over, Flint's bright green eyes were looking directly into mine. I jumped a little, startled.

"'It's okay,' Flint whispered, wrapping his arm around my waist. 'You're so beautiful when you sleep. I couldn't resist coming back here with you any longer.' He pushed my hair out of my eyes.

"My heart was pounding. I had never been that close to a man before. I didn't feel in any way comfortable with Flint in that moment."

Georgia stood slowly and waved her hand for me to sit. "I'm tired, Meaghan. Noah will be home soon.

I want to get something fixed up for him. I'll see you tomorrow." She walked toward the sink, turning on the faucet.

"Georgia, what happened? It just can't end there. I mean, I have half a page filled for the day. All it's missing is the end."

Georgia said nothing, just continued washing a dish in the sink already overloaded with soap.

I threw my notebook and pen into my bag and stood angrily. I stopped at the kitchen entry before turning around. "You asked me to write this story, Georgia, not the other way around. You have me here all day at my full disclosure. I expect the same from you. No more cliffhangers, Georgia. What happened with Flint? Finish the night."

Georgia continued scrubbing the white dish.

"Georgia, what—"

Before I could ask again, Georgia threw the dish down into the stainless steel sink. Water splashed onto the gray tile. "He raped me! He raped me, and he left me on the side of the highway that night." Georgia looked wild, full of rage.

I just stood there. Georgia's eyes were filling with tears. I took a step forward to comfort her, and she yelled, "There's your ending, journalist. You have your entertainment for tonight. Go home."

I couldn't muster up any words. I left Georgia in her kitchen crying over her sink.

Chapter 5

When I drove home that night I was welcomed by Noah, who stood smiling by his truck while I got out of the car.

"Hey, what are you doing here?"

Noah pulled out a handful of wild flowers; the purple and yellow mixture was tied with brown string. "I saw these just bloomed, a whole field behind the junkyard. I thought of you when I saw them. I hope you like them. I had a whole crew of guys giving me hell over picking flowers today." Noah smiled, and I laughed.

I took the small bundle, and my smile faded quickly after looking into his bright eyes. I had just left his sickly mother crying. How could I stand there and accept flowers from the sweetest guy on earth like nothing happened? And yet after coming to that realization, I took the flowers and ended the night abruptly, leaving another Harvest member in discomfort.

My mother was in the kitchen putting away dinner leftovers. She had fixed me a large plate and hid it in the microwave to keep warm. My father was, as was his custom, sitting in his chair watching something dealing with archery, and Cassie and my brother were out again on some college adventure.

"Meaghan, I made gravy for those potatoes if you want. It's on the top self." My mother was always a considerate woman.

I was hungry, but when I got to the table, after a few bites, I mostly played with my food. I was still thinking about Georgia. She is such an amazing woman who trusted me enough to tell me her story. Why did I have to push it? I swirled another green bean across the plate through my mashed potatoes and lifted it to my mouth, sighing.

"Meaghan, how's that writing of yours going?" My mother sat across from me with her hand under her chin.

"Fine, it's a great story to be a part of." I smiled loosely to distract my mother from my frowns.

"I'm glad to hear it. You know I always knew you'd be a writer, ever since you were, oh three or four." My mother smiled.

"How?" I asked, taking a sip of apple juice.

"Well, you would write small stories all the time. I would buy you a coloring book, and you would have a story for each picture you colored." She laughed. "I would have to say the stories were better than the pictures."

I laughed. I believe every mother knows best, even when we stubborn children think otherwise. "Thanks, Mom, I needed a pick me up."

She made her way to my side of the table and kissed my forehead. "I know you did, honey."

I stood in the shower after dinner. The hot water ran down my back. The showerhead was turned on pulsate, giving me a sort of hot massage. The aroma of my lemon body wash filled the whole bathroom; it was beyond soothing. For a moment I forgot all about Georgia, all about the secrets, and all about my financial problems and the fact that my mother felt she had a second daughter. I began feeling sleepy and decided it was time to get out. I dried my hair, slipped on an old softball shirt, and fell onto my bed. Within minutes I fell into a deep sleep.

I awoke to a pounding on the back door. No one ever knocks on the back, because they'd have to climb over our fence, and it's only an entrance to the basement. I jumped and slowly walked over to the door, suspicious. Then I thought it might be my brother who got locked out again. I opened the door. It was Noah. He stood at the door, furious.

"Noah what's wrong?" I asked.

He invited himself in, storming to the opposite side of the room. "How could you?" he screamed.

"How could I what?"

"My mother is dead. You knew it was going to happen, and you didn't tell me?"

I gasped. "Georgia's dead? She can't be. I was just there, she—"

"You left her there distraught, and she collapsed." Noah grabbed me by my throat, lifting me off my feet. I couldn't breathe. "She's dead because of you." I heard those words repeating as I slowly slipped out of consciousness.

I sat straight up in my bed, sweating, gasping for air. I had only been dreaming, of course. Feeling dizzy, I lay my head back on to the pillow and sobbed. I felt as if I were a virus, destroying people in silence. I had to see Georgia first thing in the morning. I had to convince her to tell Noah now. I was already wanting more than friendship from him, and I suspected he did also, but I couldn't begin any type of relationship with a secret. For the rest of the night I barely slept. I stared at the wildflowers in the tiny blue vase Noah had picked for me. I longed for tomorrow to come in hopes this would all be settled and everything would be fine. I also dreaded tomorrow, because I knew in reality nothing ever went how I planned it to.

I got coffee and churros as the beginning of an apology. I had never gotten out of bed and moved that fast, determined on getting to one place. When I arrived at Georgia's, Noah was just pulling out, and we waved as we passed each other. Georgia was still standing at the door when I got into the driveway. I pulled my messenger bag over my head and straightened it on my shoulder. I had full intentions of writing today. I grabbed the café box and two coffees and walked to the screen door to see Georgia smiling.

"Hey, Georgia," I said, handing her one coffee.

"Are those apple strudel churros?" She laughed. "Come on in."

While walking toward the kitchen, I began apologizing, "Georgia, about yesterday. I didn't have any right to push—"

Georgia stopped me almost immediately. "Nonsense, I don't want to hear any more of an apology from you. You were right. You are a professional writer, and I promised full disclosure at the beginning. I didn't give it to you last night, and I'm sorry."

I was shocked. Georgia was in a great mood and was ready to continue where we had left off.

"Georgia, I want to talk about something else, but after today's session, okay?" I grimaced at the thought.

"Okay, honey, you're the writer." Georgia served the churros on to the tiny white plates I was accustomed to seeing and poured hazelnut into the black coffee I had gotten her, swirling it into a smooth coco brown. I pulled out my tablet and two pens, just in case one went dry on me. I scribbled a tiny blue circle into the left corner, testing the first pen.

"So I was alone on the side of the highway, sobbing and watching Flint's car speed into Vegas for as far as I could see. Then there was nothing, no headlights. The stars were my only source of light, and I just sat there, hoping someone would come by and take me into town so I could meet my aunt on time. I sat there for hours, crying, shaking in fear, and thinking the most awful scenarios. I really thought I would be there for days. This road was different from others I had been on. Every couple of minutes anywhere else I would see a car. Here I was and I saw no one.

"Three, maybe four hours had passed. I was so tired, but I didn't want to close my eyes and miss anyone. It became more and more difficult, though, to keep my head from falling and my eyes shutting. Somewhere between all that time, I had dozed off, dreaming of a wild coyote chasing me out here. I awoke breathing heavily and crying. Flint had put all that nonsense in my head earlier that day, telling me about all the plain animals he had heard of. "'Coyotes were vicious, tore a man right out of his car and ate him whole while he slept,' he said.

"Not long after I had wakened from that gnarly nightmare, I thought I heard a motor. I stood, but saw nothing and sat back down on my suitcase, which had begun to cave in a little upon my sitting on it."

Georgia took another churro from the box. I was so busy writing I hadn't even taken one bite of mine.

"I thought I heard it again, and again I stood up. This time I saw a light, but just one. I waved my hands and jumped up and down to this man on a motorcycle. He wore a black leather jacket and a white helmet and black Ray Ban glasses. He passed by me with such speed I jumped back quite far.

"'Wait! Wait! Please come back!' I yelled, and just when I got discouraged, I kicked my suitcase and tears began streaming down my face.

"I saw him turn swiftly and brake in front of me. I clapped my hands. 'Oh, thank you, thank you so much for stopping. I need a ride I've been out her by myself all night, and I haven't seen any cars, no one. I have an appointment I have to make in Las Vegas tomorrow. Could you please, please give me a lift? I won't be any trouble, sir,' I begged this man. I was so thankful to see another person, I couldn't speak without crying.

"The man took off his glasses, revealing the bluest eyes I had ever seen. He asked me if I had ever ridden a motorcycle before. I shook my head no, and he told me to tie my case around the back and to hold on. I sat budged in between my suitcase and his leather jacket. I was in room to complain about space, so I held his waist, and we were off.

"'What's your name, kid?'

"'Georgia, Georgia Harvest. What's yours?'

"'Parker, Parker Wells, Nevada realtor and bro-
ker.' He reached for a card in his right jacket pocket
and handed it to me. It was blue with yellow letters
that said "Parker Bros. Reality," and in the center was
Parker, a man in his fifties in a gray suit standing with
a map of Nevada in his hands and a white smile on his
tanned face.

"'That's very nice,' I said. 'You're not in the market,
are you?' Parker chuckled.

"'No, not at the moment, but you sure don't miss a
pitch opportunity, do you?"

"We both laughed, and he said, 'Not in this market
I don't.'

"Parker was a very fine gentleman. He handled his
bike with such ease and control it was like they were
one. I felt very safe the whole ride. When we got to the
strip, I was silent in awe. I pointed to so many buildings.
Everything was so bright and colorful, and there were
so many people in costumes walking around, smiling.
There were street performers all along the way. I saw
two men juggling sticks of fire and a lady coaching her
dog through a handstand.

"Parker laughed. 'First time you've ever seen this,
isn't it?'

"I shook my head yes, keeping my eyes on all the sights.

"'It's always nice to see someone's reaction to all this
their first time, makes a native like me appreciate seeing it every night.'

"We pulled into a small restaurant that Parker swore
had the best food and made you feel right at home, so
inside we went. It was dark, romantic, so different from

its outside surroundings. We walked through red velvet curtains into a dining area where eight or nine tables sat, each centered with a red tablecloth and a candle.

"'This looks awfully expensive sir.'

"Parker laughed. 'Nonsense. Besides, I'm paying. I don't want to hear a word in protest either. I can't remember the last time I took a beautiful woman out.'

"I said thank you, a little on edge with men because of the recent occurrence.'"

Georgia looked up at me tensely, biting her bottom lip, then continued.

"I ordered shrimp alfredo and mashed potatoes. The shrimp was bright pink when it came out steaming. The creamy alfredo sauce slipped under my mashed potatoes and soaked up all the flavor. I ate so fast. I had been so hungry for some time. I took a gulp of my ice water and looked over to Parker, who had been watching me eat.

"'You must be very hungry.' He laughed. 'I have only seen my son eat that fast after playing in the yard all day.'

"A little embarrassed, I wiped the corners of my mouth and apologized.

"'Oh no need for an apology, Georgia. I am human also. I understand. If I spent the night in the desert, I would probably eat a platter full of food. You enjoy that, darling.'

"Parker ordered chicken parmesan. Between bites he began to tell me of his late wife Margaret. She had died during the birth of their son Tanner. He pulled a black-and-white picture from his pocket. When they were younger, he said she had short brunette hair, curly, and a lovely smile.

"'She was an incredible woman. It was so difficult for me to raise our son without her. Before his birth she was the only thing that kept me stable, and after she died, that role shifted to my son. I started a realty business with my oldest brother Weston, and I've been blessed with a son, who has already began the trade. I'm a happy man, a blessed man.' He smiled and sliced another piece of chicken, while I slid his wife's picture back across the table to him and twisted my alfredo around my fork, sliding the last bite into my mouth.

"Of course as I was finished, and he still had a plate full of pasta. He pointed his fork toward me, inquiring a synopsis of my story. I told him very little, saying I left my hometown in search of a better living, a new panoramic view. I was tired of the same old place, the same old people. He laughed and told me he understood. He also told me it sounded as if I was running away from my problems.

"'Opportunity is wherever you are, Georgia.'

"I sat in silence. It was something I wouldn't fully understand until later. Parker suggested I use the phone on the bar to contact my Aunt Loretta and find a meeting place on the strip. I called my aunt, and I was so happy to hear a familiar voice. We agreed on a meeting spot by a small cigar shop Parker said he was familiar with and would be glad to take me. My aunt said she'd see me in about an hour.

"Parker pulled just around the corner into a small brick corner shop. In gold letters it read 'Cigars.' The building reminded me of something from an old western. Parker said they received a lot of business, and he asked if my aunt smoked. I said I wasn't sure. He said it's believed that the mafia used the store as a front, and he was very surprised my aunt comfortably asked me to wait for her anywhere near this place, unless of course she was affiliated with these people.

"'Are you suggesting that my elderly aunt is mafia?'

"'No, no, I meant no offense. It's just a strange thing to be out here after all the stories I've heard.'

"I sat my suitcase down and shook Parker's hand. 'I've heard entirely too many stories from too many men lately, and I don't intend on being filled with yours. It was very nice to meet you, and I am forever indebted to you.'

"'You are debt free me, dearest Georgia. Your company alone has provided me with much more joy than money ever could, thank you.' Parker looked up at the cigar shop once more before turning to his bike and strapping on his helmet. 'You be safe now, Miss Georgia.'

"I waited outside of the cigar shop for an hour, and right on schedule, I saw a yellow Volkswagen pull forward right in front of the shop. My Aunt Loretta was saying her welcomes before she even parked. When she got out she stood tall like my mother. Her hair was brown and short and curly like Margaret's, Parker's wife.

"She kissed my cheek and told me to throw my belongings in the back and wait in the car; she was going to run into the cigar shop. I noticed a long cigar in the cigarette holder still burning. I looked into the window as I slid into my seat and saw my Aunt Loretta go behind a black velvet curtain. I couldn't shake the story Parker had begun to tell me. I sat in the car for forty-five minutes waiting. I started fidgeting, wondering what she could be doing. The cigars were sold in the front of the shop.

"Just as I was about to have a nervous breakdown, my Aunt Loretta appeared out of the back into the front of the store, kissed two gentlemen on the cheek, and apologized to me for taking so long.

"'Now, sugar, you ready to come home to a nice cooked meal and a comfortable bed?' She smiled brightly, and I shook my head yes. I was on my way to another temporary home."

Chapter 6

I ate dinner with Georgia and Noah that night. Noah had made an occasion of it. He was quite the cook. He made steak, asparagus tips, and whole Russet potatoes. Georgia had a white wine in the fridge and poured glasses around the table.

"Where did you get your cooking skills from?" I asked Noah, chewing in between conversation.

He looked over to Georgia, who started chuckling and waved her hand. "I'm no cook, Noah. You learned that from those TV shows you watch all the time."

Noah blushed a little as if it was unmanly to watch a cooking network.

I laughed. "Well, either way, Noah, this is an incredible meal."

Noah grabbed my hand. "I glad you stayed for dinner."

I looked up to see Georgia's smirking face as she lifted her clear wine glass to her bare lips. I pulled my hand away slowly, smiling awkwardly, and taking another bite of potatoes.

After dinner, I insisted on doing the dishes. Noah was helping but then got a ring from my father. He needed late help moving something for a Mrs. Hudson. He said he usually would wait until the next day, but she was an elderly woman and wanted his help tonight. Noah told me he'd better go help him.

"That Mrs. Hudson can be a hassle," he said, kissing my forehead. "Thanks for coming to dinner again."

I looked into the soapy water, smiling. I felt butterflies in my stomach, and then I began to blush, realizing Georgia was still in the room and had seen everything. I turned around to her, smiling.

"I haven't seen him do a hop skip and a jump out that door ever!" She laughed. "And since you've been here I haven't seen you smile at water as much as you are right now." Georgia clapped her hands as if she had just figured out some great mystery. "So are you going to go out with him?"

"Georgia!" I yelled as if it were the most appalling thing. "He's your son. This is a strictly professional thing. I can't believe you'd suggest something… Why, did he say something about taking me on a date?"

Georgia's laughter flooded the room. "He's been talking about you here, there, everywhere. He likes you a lot. Who knows what'll become of it. Time with tell all, honey." Georgia sipped the last drop of her white wine. "Oh what was it that you wanted to discuss earlier?"

I turned to Georgia who sat smiling on her chair, twirling a small piece of hair around her finger. When she let go a whole bundle fell on to her lap. She picked it up and held it for a moment.

I dried off my hands and said, "It was nothing."

She threw the bundle of hair into the white trash can beside her and said she was going to call it a night. I went to hug her good-bye. She waved me away.

"I'll cry if you touch me. I'll just see you tomorrow, Meaghan. Goodnight."

I pulled in behind our house to avoid anyone seeing me out front. I just sat in my car and cried for a good fifteen minutes. The look on Georgia's face while she held up her hair. I could tell she hadn't even prepared herself for anything that would happen these next months. She was already noticeably thinner. How would she hide losing her hair? And Noah, how could she tell him?

I looked in my mirror and wiped the mascara streaks from under my eyes, which were now puffy and red. I shut the car door as quietly as possible and unlocked the back door, taking me directly to my bedroom. I heard Noah's voice in the kitchen, of course, and my father's, and to my surprise Bry was up there too. I heard my mother shuffling around, probably serving drinks to everyone. she was always excited when there was company, like she had never seen another human being.

I threw my bag against the nightstand and flopped onto the futon. My mother knocked on the door. She must have heard me walking around down here.

"Meaghan? Meaghan, Noah is here. Are you going to come up?"

I lay there non responsive. I had no intentions on speaking or moving anywhere.

"Meaghan? Are you down there?"

I heard my father's voice now. "Of course she's down there. The cars around back."

"Why would she park out back?"

I yelled up the stairs, intervening between my father's sarcastic observances and my mother's continuous questions. "I'm down here. I'm not coming up. Just tell Noah I said hi!"

Again my mother knocked. "Meaghan are you still down there?"

"Of course she's still down there. She just answered you."

"Well, I was just checking."

I stood and marched up the steps. I was tired of hearing my parents arguing. "I don't feel like conversing tonight. I've had a busy day, and I'm tired now. Goodnight, Noah." Before there were any ifs, ands, or buts I shut the door and made my way back down the steps and onto my bed.

A little after ten when Noah left and everyone went to bed, I crept upstairs into the kitchen, reaching for the little bite muffins my mother always buys. I didn't see them anywhere. I looked in every cabinet, and then I heard something, so I flicked on the lights.

"Dad?"

My father had been sitting in his chair with the box of little bites in his hand. He stood up, handed me the box, taking one more muffin, and said, "Goodnight."

I laughed as he walked up the stairs, his hands in his robe pockets. I turned on the TV back in my room and ate until I was at the bottom of the box. I Love Lucy re-runs were on. I thought of Georgia as I laughed. She spoke highly of this show and The Honeymooners, saying they were her brother's favorites.

I reached for my phone and snapped a picture of the TV screen. I added it to the Georgia Harvest album, titling it Day Fifteen. I slid through some of the photos I had taken so far, stopping at the ones Georgia had taken of Noah and I at dinner the other night. I had to admit I looked very happy in the pictures, and Noah's smile was breathtaking. My favorite was after dinner before Noah had left. We were just pouring dish liquid into the sink, and he had gathered soapy bubbles and put them on his chin. I laughed, reliving the moment.

Then I thought about Georgia, as I often did. I remembered her saying, "All we've got is memories." I thought of her lifting up each of the pictures she had shown me, breathing in deeply then out. I remember the pictures of Flint standing with his guitar by a gas station sign squinting at the hot sun; the two boys, Tobias and Tyler, running around a field while Candice sat on a wooden bench smiling brightly at the camera; and the picture of Parker and Georgia holding on for her life on his motorcycle, her suitcase holding her in place, the whole Las Vegas strip in the background.

"What a life," I murmured. I shut off my phone and sat it on my nightstand. Lily jumped on to the corner of my bed, her black hair flying everywhere, as I laid my head on my pillow and called it a night.

—❦—

I heard knocking on the back door. I hit my phone, which read 7:35. It was much earlier than I was accustomed to waking. I grabbed for my Steve Madden glasses and threw my comforter off. I walked to the door, shooing Lily away, who sat curiously at the door.

"Noah?" My eyes widened as I reminisced on my nightmare. "What are you doing here?" I asked as he stood there, eyeing me up and down. I admitted I wasn't the most glorifying thing in the morning.

"No, no." He laughed. "You looked great. Can I come in? I wanted to talk to you about something."

My heart was pounding out of my chest. Georgia must have told him after last night.

Noah walked in, looking around touching the covers on the two pool tables. "Ah, this must be the pool hall your father was speaking about."

I shut the door as he turned toward me. "Yeah, I pretty much crashed in the middle of his work." I clasped my hands together nervously, hoping this small talk wouldn't last much longer.

"What made you move back? From what I've gathered you despise little ole Franklin city." Noah laughed while crossing his arms and leaning on the first pool table.

I frisked my bun and shooed Lily away again, who was standing on the pool table sniffing Noah. "I don't despise Franklin anymore. I never really did. It's just I didn't feel it had anything to offer for journalism, and besides, did my brother tell you that?"

Noah laughed again, his pearly whites beaming, which made me run to the bathroom and brush my morning breath away. When I came back out, Noah had the television on and Lily on his lap, who acted as if no one ever gave her an ounce of attention. A Twilight Zone marathon was on.

"I didn't know you were into these old shows. I'm quite the fan myself." I folded my bed back to its futon stage and asked Noah to sit. "So why are you up so early?" I said, motioning to my phone, which now read 8:02.

Noah brushed some of Lily's hair from his green military style jacket. I picked her up and put her on the floor. "She sheds a lot."

"I noticed. She's a good cat though."

I sat beside Noah, grabbing for my open box of Cheese Nips, which were now partly stale, and pushed the box toward him, offering him some.

"No thanks, I ate breakfast. I wanted to talk to you about something that's been on my mind lately."

"Noah, I know, and I understand if you don't want to be friends. I should have told you from the start."

He grabbed my hand. "I should have said something too, Meaghan. I don't want to just be friends anymore. I'm so glad you feel the same. Can I pick you up for dinner tonight around eight?"

I tilted my head like a dog would in confusion. I shook my head yes and smiled as he stood.

"Great, I'll see you tonight then." Noah kissed my forehead and walked out the door.

I plopped on my futon, screaming into the pillow.

Chapter 7

After my morning therapy session with my pillow, I got a quick shower and sat in front of my vanity, brushing the many tangles from my hair. I looked at myself in the mirror. I had a date tonight with someone I genuinely liked, which had not happened in some time. I let my hair air dry and used some of the new makeup I purchased with Cassie, who explained makeup is not as scary I as I thought. She was a sweet girl. I could see why my family liked her and why she was a good match for my brother.

I grabbed a stippling brush and dipped it into some foundation, patting it into my oily skin. I swirled another brush into some powder, gliding it in circular motions across my face. I sat there looking into the mirror, admiring how I looked after some weeks of self-restoration. I had done more these last weeks than I had in three years in New York. I looked over to my phone. It was afternoon now, and I had to make my way to Georgia's to start on our day. It would be something to take my mind off of tonight.

"Well look at you!" Georgia was standing next to the door.

I had on a long floral maxi dress with a black leather jacket sitting in the front seat, preparing for the cool breeze tonight.

"Noah's not here, is he? We have plans tonight, and this is what I intended on wearing. I don't want him to see until later."

Georgia smiled. "No, he's long gone." She opened the door. "So you'ens have a date?"

"I'm not sure if I would call it a date just yet. He just asked me to dinner."

"It's a date!" Georgia poured a glass of tea for me, and she sat down across from me as custom. "You got to treat it like a date. He thinks it's a date. It's a date, honey, no question he likes you enough to ask you out. It's a date." Georgia hardly took a breath.

"Okay, it's a date. I'm just nervous is all." I wrapped my hair up into a small bun. It was hotter in the day now.

Georgia stood to push the windows above the sink open, and she flicked a switch by the refrigerator, turning the white dusty fan on above the table. "You've got nothing to worry about. You look stunning, and you'll forget all about being nervous and just have fun. That's not until later. You've got the whole day to prepare." Georgia sat sipping her tea, saying it needed more sugar.

I grabbed for my pen, and we picked back up where we left off.

"I woke up the next morning. I can't really remember the ride to my aunt's home. I was so tired I slept the whole way. John, my aunt's husband, who was a tall and handsome gentleman with thick, bushy eyebrows, picked me out of the car and took me into a bedroom they had set aside for me. I hadn't slept that good in sometime. When I saw John that morning, he was pouring coffee. He turned and nodded his head. He had such a stern look. The sunlight peering through the yellow daisy-covered curtains above the sink revealed the bags under his eyes and the sunspots, showing signs of hard work.

"'I'm off to the store. I've got a few errands to do today. I'll see you ladies this evening.' John kissed my forehead and welcomed me to the house. Then he walked to the eat-in counter my aunt was sitting at, kissed her on the forehead, and placed a white envelope on the bar for her. He walked out the door, and it was just my aunt Loretta and I.

"'Are you hungry, Georgia?' She stood and lifted a red lid from a glass bowl. 'It's potatoes, eggs, bacon, and onions with a little cheese on top. There's juice in the fridge if you like.' She sat back down and continued to read the paper and pick at her Danish.

"'Thank you, and thank you for letting me stay here.'

"'Oh hush now. You're my niece, and you may stay as long as you like. Plus, it'll be nice to have company at the store.' She smiled, wiping the sides of her mouth. She looked at her watch. 'We've got to be there by nine, so as soon as you're finished, go on and clean up.'

"'Is that when you open, nine everyday?' I asked, chewing.

"Loretta picked up one of her long skinny cigars. 'I open when I please. I have to meet with someone there today is all.' She blew out a cloud of smoke. 'Eat up now.'"

Georgia sipped her tea once more, insisting it needed more sugar.

"So I came out of my room with a dress on and gloves, a pair Candice had given me when she dropped me off in New Mexico.

"My Aunt Loretta laughed. 'Lord, child, I will take you shopping in the plaza today. You're in Vegas now. You need to dress like it, especially when your with me.'

"I looked up and down at my clothes. I agreed they probably weren't high fashion, but Loretta insisted they were worse than second-hand clothes. We walked into the jewelry shop at nine sharp. She threw her keys on the counter by the register and told me to look around and get a feel for the place.

"'I'll show you how to work the register. It's real simple. You'll be here all day as will I. If I have to run anywhere, you stay. You have access to everything, and at the end of each night I'll pay you according to the hours we were opened. Got everything, hun?'

"I shook my head yes. I was eager to start a job and save my money up again. I walked around the store, running my fingers over everything. The whole time I had my eye on a bright red velvet curtain. It reminded me of the ones in the restaurant Parker had taken me to. My aunt said it led to the upstairs of the building and that I was not to go up there.

"'It's just a room with a few tables John and his friends play cards at, nothing special to see anyhow.'

"Still my curiosity was heightened enough to know that one day I'd just have to see about those tables. A few minutes after we had arrived, I was hanging earrings on a plastic display case on the counter. Loretta was taking inventory on some new items she got.

"She turned her head and smiled. 'Well hell, Bill, if I knew you were going to be late, I wouldn't have been on time neither.'

"'Oh please, don't give me hell this early, Lo. I'm ten minutes late.'"

"Ten minutes today, twenty tomorrow. Bill.' My aunt set her clipboard down. 'I hope you were smart enough to bring what you were supposed to.'

"'I have it, Loretta. I haven't been late with my payments yet, and you know it.' She smiled. 'Come upstairs now, Bill.' She turned to me as a small group of older women walked in. 'Hello, ladies,' she began. 'Look all around. We've got some new items in. If you have any questions, Georgia will take care of you.' She winked at me and headed up the steps, closing the curtain behind her.

"I was ringing the older ladies up. They each already had rings on every finger and multiple necklaces and pins on. They bought so many little boxes with earrings and bracelets and more beads to add to their collection. I had almost finished ringing them up when my aunt was walking down the steps. It had been a good twenty minutes, and the man she called Bill was red in the face, containing all his anger.

"'I'll see you soon now, Bill.' She smirked as if she was a child with a ball. The ball was the man, and she was the mischievous child. He walked toward the door.

"'Oh Bill, don't be rude now. This is my niece Georgia. She'll be here for some time, so please pay your dues to her.'

"'Nice to me to you, miss.' He waved to me hurriedly. 'Can I go now?'

"'Don't be ridiculous, Bill, of course you can.'

"He left, and my aunt helped me wrap the ladies' orders and get them out the door. My aunt was back to her inventory, and I was polishing display cases.

"'Who was that man?' I finally blurted out. 'He's just and old customer. He was indebted to me, came to pay off some things.' She continued scribbling down inventory.

"'Oh, why was he indebted to you?'

She set her board down and turned to me. "Georgia, you see that building across the street? It's a deli, but John and I, we co-own that building, and the building beside it, and the next eight beside those. Bill the man, you seen this morning, rents that deli off of John, our partner, and me. He couldn't afford his place, and I allowed him to stay with some minor adjustments, and he came to pay off his debt.' She was back to her board again.

"'That's amazing to have all of that, Aunt Loretta. Whose your partner?'

"'Georgia darling, it's rude to ask too many questions.'

"'I'm sorry. I am always curious, that's all," I said, setting the duster down.

"'It's fine, honey. I'll be closing in an hour, so finish up and get ready to go shopping.'

"We walked just down the plaza to a pink building called Madame Isle's. Just inside the door stood two showgirl mannequins, and behind the register a large woman, maybe three hundred pounds, with bright yellow eye shadow and bright pink blush. She wore a bright orange dress and had even brighter red hair.

"She stretched her sagging arms out. 'Lo Lo! I haven't seen you for some time! Come in.'

"Hello, Isle, this is my niece Georgia, and she is in need of a Las Vegas makeover. Whatever she wants. I'll just take the total off of what you owe.'

"Isle smiled as my aunt proposed to deduct her bill. 'Come on, child, look at whatever you want. Try on whatever you desire!' She wrapped a feather scarf around my neck.

"I tried on dresses and skirts and hats, and when I was finished I had gotten three skirts, twelve blouses, three dresses, and two hats. My aunt stopped off at a barbeque spot and picked up a few things for dinner. She swore she hated cooking, and that if there was a home-cooked meal, John made it.

"'I'm sorry I wasn't there for your mother's funeral, Georgia. I couldn't do it, you know. When I went to Marlene's, I hated seeing everyone so upset, and well, I just couldn't do it. I sent Elton some money to take care of y'all for a while.'

"I turned my head quickly in surprise. 'You did?'

"'Well of course I did. Elton never mentioned it, did he?'

"I shook my head no.

"'Isn't that just like him. Well, I sent your brother money to help pay for anything he had to, whether it was for the house or for the funeral. I loved your mother. She was the only sister I had, my best friend.' She began tearing up while lighting another cigar.

"'It's okay, Aunt Loretta. My mom would be very grateful for you letting me stay with y'all and giving me a job.'

"She put her hand on mine. 'It's my pleasure.'

"John was pulling in when we did. Once inside, my aunt pulled out chicken, biscuits, coleslaw, and tea. It was a fine meal.

"'What'd you think of the store, Georgia?' John looked at me with his stern eyes, but he was smiling and grabbed for the tea.

"'I liked it just fine. There was lots of beautiful jewelry,' I said, breaking a biscuit in half and spreading jam across as it steamed.

"'Well, I'm glad you liked it. You'll be good working for us, Lo, and I have business to take care of on a daily basis, so it'll be nice to have a trusted cashier working for us.' He took another bite of chicken, licking the sauce from his dried lips.

"'Oh I'm grateful to you. It'll be nice saving money up again.'

"John nodded his head in approval. 'It's nice to save up your hard-earned money then invest it into something you can make more of a profit off.'

"Loretta smiled, taking a sip of tea then a puff of her cigar. 'John, don't bore her to death about business and money. She was pushing buttons all day. Let's just enjoy our food.'

"John smiled and took a gulp of tea. 'You comfortable here, Georgia? You're welcomed to stay as long as you need.'

"I smiled and said thank you. I helped clean the plates and silverware after dinner and walked down to my bedroom, hanging my new clothes in the green wallpapered closet.

"Loretta knocked on the door. 'I just wanted to tell you, sug, we'll be there by eleven tomorrow, so go on and sleep in if you'd like.' She walked toward the closet and kissed my forehead. 'It's good to have you here, Georgia. Goodnight.'

"I said goodnight and sat on the edge of the bed. I felt welcomed, like I had felt when my mother would come in after work and kiss me on the forehead. I thought about Elton, about calling him and telling him I was all right and asking him about the money my aunt had sent to him. Then I shook my head. He probably wouldn't talk to me, and if he did, he would yell and criticize anything I found enjoyment in. I wanted so badly, though, to lay under the covers and hear my mother's footsteps coming into my room, the white door creaking as she tiptoed toward the bed trying not to wake me, her soft lips on my forehead, and the comforter hitting the bottom of my chin as she pulled it over me. Those were the memories I never wanted to forget.

"I lay in bed that night thinking about what Parker had said. The word mafia scrolled through my head. I just couldn't picture my Aunt Loretta in the mafia or anything like it. Her and my uncle were just average hardworking people, but I still couldn't shake the feeling that all my answers would lie behind that red velvet curtain."

Chapter 8

I left Georgia's and headed home. It was nearly eight now, and I wanted to be there before one of my parents saw his headlights and invited Noah in, questioning him about what we were going to do and where we were going to go.

I pulled into the driveway, and I didn't see his truck yet. I pulled down the visor and looked in the mirror while I hurriedly ran the mascara wand through my stubby lashes. When I saw his headlights coming down the road, I instantly got butterflies I had been shooing away all day. I stood beside my car, grabbing for the leather jacket, shielding my body from the cool breeze my father had predicted for this evening. I got right into his truck.

"I don't want to cause a scene with my family, so if you could just keep driving…"

He laughed. "You look beautiful tonight. You look different, but beautiful never the less."

I pushed back a short piece of hair and looked into the right mirror as he looked left, watching for traffic.

"So where are we going?" I asked.

"This small place up here. My friend Pete owns it. I made dinner arrangements there so we'd just get right in. I know how everyone in Franklin likes to dine out on Fridays."

I smiled, thinking about my family in the past eating out on weekends. My brother always wanted to go to Pete's pizzeria.

Noah walked over to my door and opened it. It was like a breath of fresh air contrary to any guy I've ever gone out with, who just got out and walked into the restaurant, expecting me to keep up.

"Thank you, sir."

"My pleasure, ma'am."

Noah took my hand, and we walked into the pizzeria, which was crowded. I saw a few familiar faces, and Noah was welcomed like the president. We pushed past all the booths straight to the back, where the wooden table was covered with a red cloth, unlike the others, and centered with two tall white candles, wax sliding down the sides, holstered by silver holders.

"Wow, Noah, this is beautiful." I smiled as I slide across the cool wooden seat.

He sat across from me. "Well, I had to do something to make it look special. I know this isn't the finest dining you've ever had probably, especially living in New York and all."

I reached over to touch his hand. "It's perfect, incomparable to anything yet." I smiled.

Noah and I decided to split a broccoli and cheese pizza with breadsticks and a small pasta salad; it was delicious. I had forgotten I was even on a date. All the butterflies had disappeared, and we were just talking about so much. I opened up more in that moment with him than I could ever remember, and then a knot of intuition twisted my stomach. I felt sick and uneasy.

"That's incredible, so you said before you stopped writing, and now you're writing again. How did my mom inspire you to do that? I mean, I think my mother's an amazing woman, but to you she was just a stranger." Noah grabbed his breadstick, dipped it in the melted garlic butter, and just sat there so interested, so oblivious to everything.

I awkwardly began to lie, "Well, she brought up an old article I wrote some years back, and she told me how good it was and…" I sipped my ice water. "And it just motivated me to write some more stuff, so how is your job?" I smiled and gulped more water as if I had just ran a mile.

Noah looked at me suspiciously and then shook his head, laughing, "Meaghan, do I make you nervous?"

"Yes!" I shouted, in hopes that he would accept this excuse for my strange all-of-a-sudden behavior.

Noah grabbed my hands. "I don't do this…ever, but I really like you, and I want to see you again after this if you'd like."

I shook my head yes.

"Great, I just want to take this as slow as possible so you're not nervous around me or anything."

———

I unlocked the door like I was being chased by a serial killer. Noah kicked the door shut with his heel, and we continued to kiss. He pulled off my leather jacket, and I kicked off my heels.

I put my finger up to his lips. "Shhh, we have to be quiet. Everyone's in bed."

Noah smiled. "Right, so let's get you in bed."

I chuckled. I never did this. I said that several times, and I could tell he never did this either, because he mentioned it several times as well. He covered my mouth with his hand and kissed my cheek as he finished. I asked him to stay, and he said gladly. He held me so tightly that night, I felt protected, safe, free to close my eyes and dream, something I hadn't been exposed to before.

I awoke stretching my arms out wide. Lily was sitting in front of my face as usual, and I felt an arm wrap around my waist and pull me in.

"Good morning, beautiful." Noah kissed the back of my neck. He stood and pulled his jeans up with him. "Get dressed. I'll take you for breakfast."

I grabbed a pair of distressed jeans, the only pair I had that fit me well enough. I pulled my hair in a high ponytail and grabbed my glasses as we snuck out the door. When we got to his truck, my brother was standing there with two buckets of dirt.

"Ohh, late night!"

Noah got in the truck, and I punched Bryan's shoulder. "Say anything, and I will kill you."

"Don't worry about it," he said, walking toward the garden pit my mother had started around the porch.

We drove to the café we had been accustomed to getting coffee from. I ordered an onion bagel, and Noah ordered croissants and coffee. He motioned toward a table in the corner. The seats were tall like those at a bar, and wooden. I couldn't stop smiling. I would look up and smile and look back and smile. It was probably the most nauseating thing to see from the other customers' view, but I hadn't been happy like this...ever.

"You want a ride back home, or are you going to my mom's?"

Noah had looked down at his silver watch and said he had to get back to work. I took the offer of a ride back to my place. I needed to get all my materials together before I headed over to Georgia's and started writing for today.

Georgia Harvest Challenge: Day Seventeen was Noah and I's breakfast at the corner café.

"That's a good one," Noah said.

I titled it in my phone. "Yes, so I forever remember the deliciousness of that stale onion bagel." We laughed, and he kissed me on the forehead just before I hopped out of his truck and made my way around back to my room.

My father surprised me around back as he was loading small boxes into his moving van. "Well, you can't use the front door anymore?"

"Of course I can. I just have been using this one more. What are all those boxes?"

"I wish you would use the front more, Meaghan. Are we so bad that you can't bare to see us when you come home at night? And it's just empty inventory boxes for the store." My father looked at me as if he still wanted an answer to the first statement.

"Sorry, I'll use the front door more. I've got to go. I'm late now."

"Yeah, I'm a little behind schedule too." My father continued tossing his boxes in the van, and I ran inside, grabbed my messenger bag, and was back out the door and into the jeep.

I walked up on Georgia's porch.

"Meaghan, is that you out there?" Georgia was yelling from the kitchen.

"Hey, Georgia."

"Come in, honey. I'm out here."

I entered the kitchen where Georgia was sitting, stirring a green pitcher of her sweet tea. I sat my bag down on the table across from her and grabbed two glass mugs from the cabinet.

"There's a turkey sandwich on the second shelf in the fridge there for you and chips in the cabinet. Why, Meaghan, you're glowing."

I rubbed my cheek. I could feel my face getting hot.

"I was going to have Noah run to the store for me early this morning, but I knocked on his door, and he never answered."

I had my back turned toward Georgia as I was slowly pulling the sandwich she had made for me from the fridge.

"You know I don't remember seeing his truck all morning, and I stayed up as late as I could, but he didn't come home."

I poured a glass of tea, standing beside the table. Georgia's eyes peered over her gold-rimmed glasses.

"Oh?" I remarked as if I was focusing so hard on pouring the tea.

"Didn't you two have some kind of date thing last night?"

I sunk into my chair. "So, Georgia, we should pick back up where you left off."

"Did he stay the night?" Georgia smiled.

I continued, "You had just fallen asleep at your aunt's."

"Did you have fun? At least answer that."

I dropped my pen with frustration. "Yes, Georgia, I had fun for the most part. Can we please focus on you?"

Georgia pushed her glasses back, smiling. "Okay, journalist.

"So I had worked at the jewelry store for a few months. Nothing extremely out of the ordinary happened, and I hadn't seen behind that curtain yet, but every week my aunt would have some visitor that supposedly owed her money. My aunt and uncle never mentioned anything more about the work outside the jewelry shop. My questions ceased, but my curiosity did not!" She raised her fist.

"It was in the middle of November now, near Thanksgiving. I was ringing up a customer one afternoon, and my aunt was doing inventory. My uncle John happened to be there that day hanging some new displays on the back wall. A middle-aged woman wearing a long black skirt and white blouse burst into the store and fell to her knees by the door. She was sobbing. It was quite a ruckus. My uncle dropped his hammer, and my aunt dropped her board. I was just in the middle of a conversation with a nice blonde woman, who was purchasing earrings for her seventeen-year-old daughter's birthday. She had cut the conversation short, grabbing her bag and sliding out the door at the sight of the crazed woman.

"'Bill, my Bill, Bill!' She cried louder as my aunt rushed to the door to lock it and flip the closed sign.

"My uncle went to the woman's side. 'What happened to Bill, Cynthia? What happened to him?' My uncle sat in front of her, both of his knees on the floor, his hands on the tops of her shoulders.

"My aunt looked up at me amongst the chaos and whispered to my uncle. They grabbed Cynthia by her arms, helping her stand, and coaxed her as they pushed the red velvet curtain aside and walked her up the stairs.

"My aunt came back down to pull the curtain across. Smiling, she said, 'Nothing to worry about, Meaghan, just an over-hysterical friend of ours. Count the money in the register for today. We'll most likely be going home early.'

"I shook my head yes as she dropped the curtain to the floor, and I heard her black kitten heels clicking up the staircase. The woman's cries were so loud; I was convinced if that had been a steel door instead of a curtain I would still hear her sobbing. I hit the register door open and began counting the little that we had made today. Every time I'd get halfway through, I'd lose my focus and just stare at the curtain. I heard my uncle several times pleading for the woman to 'be quiet' and 'hush a little.' I heard my aunt's heels circling the floor. Something was wrong.

"When I finally had gotten the money counted, ten maybe fifteen minutes had passed. Things were a little quieter now, and I heard more low voices instead of cries. I was entirely fed up and entirely too curious to just hold my position by the register, so I tiptoed over to the curtain. I made sure to stand to the far right of it to avoid my shadow being seen through the middle, even though the curtain looked thick enough to hide it.

"'Bill called me from the deli saying he had just finished putting all the meat away, and he had one more stop to make before he came home, that was around 7:30. An hour later Bill wasn't home, so I figured he might have stopped off to have a beer or two, because he does that once in a while, but then eleven o'clock rolled around, and I was panicking, because Billy's always been home before eleven, even before ten! I called the deli, and the phone just rang and rang and rang.' Cynthia began to cry again.

"My uncle's soft voice calmed her somewhat. 'Go on. What then?' he whispered.

"'So then I told myself that maybe today felt extra exhausting for Bill, and maybe there was a possibility that he had more than a couple of beers, and maybe he went back to the deli and passed out.'

"My aunt's voice broke in, 'Has Bill ever done something like that?'

"Cynthia cried louder. 'No! Never! But I told myself that so I could sleep. I decided I'd drive in to the deli in the morning and that it would all be all right.' Her cries were high pitched, and she began sniffling louder and blowing her nose harder.

"I was so intrigued I put my ear right against the curtain to hear everything.

"'I woke up this morning around 9:30 or 9:45. The phone was ringing in the kitchen, and I thought it was Bill, so I ran to the phone, and it was Alonzo, the boy that works in the deli at the counter with Bill. He called me from across the street. He said the doors were locked and that Bill had always had the door open for him at nine so he could come in and help get the store ready for the day. I asked him if he was sure the doors weren't stuck or anything. He swore that he pulled on the doors several times before calling me. He told me that Bill instructed him that if those doors were ever locked and it was after nine to call me. I told Alonzo to hold tight and that I would be there in twenty minutes.'

"My foot hit the back of a display that stood off to the right of the curtain. I quickly reached to steady it, praying it wasn't a loud enough noise to halt the conversation upstairs.

"'Of course I got ready as fast as I could. I hadn't given myself the time to do my hair, so I grabbed a hat and the spare store key Bill had kept under the slow cooker in the kitchen.' There was another hard blow into a tissue, which I imagined was worn at this point.

"'I pulled up in front of the deli. Alonzo ran up beside me as I walked to the door. He told me good morning, apologized for waking me, and said he just did what Bill had told him to. I told him he did everything as he should have and thanked him. I asked him what time he and Bill closed the night before. He said around seven, because Bill had to make a last delivery, so he told him to go on home.

"'I jiggled the key in the door and pushed on the door. Alonzo followed behind me.'

"The woman began to get hysterical again.

"'What happened? Cynthia, finish what happened,' my uncle said, raising his voice a little.

"'I went behind the counter, and everything was in the ordinary, so I told Alonzo to stay in the front of the shop as I made my way to the back where Bill keeps all the meat in coolers, and there was Bill on the floor. His head was cut at the temple. Blood had dried all on the side of his face and ran in streaks onto the speckled tile.'

"I pushed my ear as close toward the conversation as I could.

"'I fell to the floor shaking him, yelling his name. I called for Alonzo to go and call for help. Bill was moaning, and I told him it would be okay.' The woman stopped to let out a deep breath. 'The emergencies came and asked me if I knew what happened. I said of course I didn't, even though I had a feeling as to what did, and they took him off to the hospital.'

"'My uncle spoke again. 'Is he all right? What was his status?'

"'He's alive, thank God. He hasn't said a word yet. The doctors told me they weren't going to push him, that all his levels show he's been severely stressed.'

"'Well,' my aunt began, 'that is good news.'

"'The woman raised her voice in anger now. 'You two! I want you to look at me and tell me that you had nothing to do with this. Tell me! I know it was either you two or that creep you work for!'

"'My uncle spoke in a firm low tone. 'Be careful whose names you go throwing around, Cynthia. Now I can assure you that Loretta and I had nothing to do with what happened to Bill, and as far as our associate goes, well I can't speak for another man, and I would advise you not to go around town in hysterics accusing anyone.'

"'I heard a chair slide. I assumed Cynthia stood. 'No John! You think I didn't think about that already? That I could be next? You know why I'm hysterical, John? Because I know. I know that whoever did this, which I have a pretty good idea, and I know you know it too, they thought that they killed my husband, and when they find out they didn't Billy is still alive and even more of a threat since there's a dozen police officers crowding his hospital bed waiting to hear what happened, you don't think they'll come back and finish him for good?'

"'Cynthia, calm down—'

"'Don't you dare tell me to calm down. My family is on a hit list, Lo! Let me ask you something. What if John didn't come home?'

"'Cynthia, stop,' I heard my uncle say.

"'What if you walked into the store and John was on the floor covered in his own blood?'

"'That's enough, Cynthia," he said again.

"'What if John was half alive in the hospital, and you knew you wouldn't be seeing him much longer?'

"My aunt calmly spoke. 'Then I would be at the hospital spending as much time with him as I could.'

"There was a long silence. I was taken aback by my aunt's cold response. I hustled over to the register as I heard footsteps descending.

"'You two are doomed.' Cynthia walked out of the store and made her way across the street.

"My aunt and uncle looked at each other and then in my direction.

"'Did you count everything?' my aunt asked.

"I shook my head yes. 'Is everything all right? She seemed quite mad.'

"'Everything is just right. Don't worry about a thing.'

"We all turned suddenly at the screeching of brakes just outside. As I lifted my head I saw Cynthia's body take flight and hit the asphalt. I gasped, and my uncle ran out the door along with others on the sidewalks.

"My aunt Loretta grabbed me and whispered, 'Jesus.'"

Georgia took a swig of tea.

"Oh my God, did she die?" I asked, always eagerly waiting for the next part.

"Well, my uncle came back into the store, and he had blood on his hands and on the bottom part of his shirt.

"'John.' My aunt held me tighter.

"'The emergencies are out there doing the best the can. Whoever hit her drove off. I'd be surprised if she made it.'

"I was in shock. I had starting crying, and my aunt told my uncle to pull the car around the back of the store so I wouldn't have to be in all the chaos out front. I had never seen anyone get hit. I couldn't imagine the pain she felt, if she felt anything at all. It all brought back memories of my sister Marlene. I couldn't help but to picture my sister dying in her automobile accident.

"We went back to Loretta's place, and she told me to go lie down, that she would fix something up to calm my nerves. I held the yellow pillow close to me. I kept running everything through my mind, especially Cynthia saying, 'You're doomed.' I heard Parker's voice and the word mafia. I felt I was on to something that I didn't want to be on to, but my curiosity would never let me forget about anything I had seen or heard. I still needed to get time alone to find out what was behind the red curtain."

Chapter 9

Georgia stood, holding onto the corner of the table, and slowly ascended. I watched her grimace in her short steps to the sink and then grab onto the counter as if she might collapse at any moment.

"How you feeling today, Georgia?"

She turned toward me and smiled. "Fine, just fine."

I wasn't convinced. "Your lying through your teeth," I said, standing with my messenger bag around my shoulder.

"So what if I am? You're the journalist. I'm the story. It's your job to write, that's all." Georgia had a stern look on her face. The shadow from the windows caught the corners of her eyes, making her look more sickly and aged.

"It's also my job to ask questions, Georgia. Look, I went out with Noah last night, and it was incredible, but every time I would start having fun, I had this little voice in the back of my head whispering, 'Liar.' How the hell am I supposed to continue to see someone I genuinely like and totally dismiss the fact that I know more about his mother than he does?"

Georgia stood tall, and as she stretched herself, her back lowered again in agony.

"Georgia, you've lost weight, and the other night, hair."

"You little witch! You think I don't know that? You think I don't see or feel myself dying? Excuse me if

I feel the need to prolong my explanation to my son about his mother dying. I don't need him catering to me every day, and I certainly don't need you in my house questioning my every move. I see how you look at me, full of pity."

"Georgia I—"

"That's why I'm waiting to tell him, because I can't stand to see that look in everyone's eyes, especially Noah's."

I stood silent.

"Please leave, and if you feel the need to worry and pity me, just come here for the money I pay you. Come here as a businesswoman, not a friend."

I had nothing more to say, so I slowly walked out the door and to my car. I threw my messenger bag onto the passenger seat.

The cash Georgia had given me for writing so far fell out of the front pocket of my bag and on to the seat. I stared at it, wondering if all this was worth what was lying in that seat.

Georgia Harvest Challenge: Day Eighteen was a stray cat I saw on my way home. It reminded me of Lily. I threw a piece of bagel I had picked up at the café at it. The cat sniffed it and ran away.

"Yeah, I don't blame you," I said aloud, throwing the whole bagel out the window.

I didn't want to go home yet, and I didn't want to go back to Georgia's, who probably despised me, and I didn't want to see Noah, because like a gentleman, he'd ask what was wrong, and I didn't have the heart to tell him another lie, and I didn't have the heart to tell him the truth.

I drove to a park by the river my dad used to take my brother and me fishing at. I walked down to a faded red picnic table we always used to sit at for the view of the whole river. I sat atop of the table and just closed my eyes, listening to the soothing water flow. It was evening now, and the sky was a darker blue. There were no clouds tonight, just stars.

"What's happening?" I whispered to myself.

"The sun is setting."

I turned quickly around to see my father carrying a fishing rod and a bait box. He sat them on the table behind me and sat beside me, looking out to the river.

"I didn't know you'd be here,"

"Oh I come here often still. Come to this same table even. It was always our spot, remember?"

I shook my head yes and felt my father's eyes on me. "

You all right, kid? You've been here and there lately. You live in the same house as I do, and I hardly see you. What's up?"

I put my elbows on my knees and held my head with my hands. "Nothing, Dad. I just got wrapped up in a project is all. I remember working for the paper. The editor told me never to get emotionally involved in any work that I do. He said it would soften my questions and distract me from my job. I understand that now. I just wish I was totally numb, Dad." I looked over to my father and then back to the river.

"I think what he said is not entirely true."

I smiled. My dad would always have kind words for us kids.

"If you were numb like you said, how could you ever write something genuine? I think you getting emotionally involved in whatever you're working on makes it that much better, because you want it to work out. You want it to be the best thing you've worked on to date, and because of that it'll be the greatest project you've ever done."

"You think so, Dad?" I said, smiling, knowing he was right.

"The best inventions we have around today are because of people who got emotionally involved in what they were doing." He picked up his fishing rod. "Look at this, for example. Some guy had been walking to a river just like this one every day with a long stick and a string with a tiny metal hook tied to the end of it. He was catching nothing, or he'd catch small fish that he'd have to throw back, because the bigger fish would break the stick or break the string and take the bait.

"He decided to create something that would beat all these faults, so day in and day out he would work on this invention. He spent time away from his family, quit his job, and hadn't seen friends in months. If that's not getting emotionally involved, I don't know what is, but the amazing thing about this story is he created this right here. It sold out in stores everywhere. It was the greatest thing he created, but he had to sacrifice things to get there. You have looking for an opportunity to write for years, you moved for the opportunity away from your family and friends, and now you've found something that you believe in, and you've been spending time away from your family, and it's the only thing you've been working on. Sounds like a great project in the works to me."

I hugged my dad. "Thanks, Dad. I really, really needed that today."

"Come on, let's get home. Your mother's probably sending a search crew out for us."

The next day I decided to stay home with my family. It was Sunday, and I knew Noah had the day off. I hoped he would stay with Georgia all day. I hadn't spent time like this with my family in years. My father sat at his chair, and my brother and I at the couch. My mom was making lunch, and Lily was propped up at the end of the couch, seeking attention from everyone.

We all ate together at the table, something I hadn't remembered doing since Bry and I were kids. Everyone was sitting around the table laughing and smiling. It's something I missed. After lunch I was feeling tired. I walked down to the basement, hit the futon, and switched the television. Within moments I was sound asleep. I heard consistent knocks on the back door that made me finally open my sleepy eyes.

I grabbed for my glasses and realized I had slept for about four hours. The knocks continued.

"Hold on!" I flipped the covers off of me and pushed Lily out of the way.

"Hey! You're here!" It was Noah, who looked nervous. He had his hands in his jean pockets and was tapping his right foot.

"Is everything okay?" I asked, holding the door only slightly open to keep the cat in.

"Yeah, well, I mean I didn't get to see you after the morning yesterday. My mom said you come over on Sunday, and I stopped by last night, but your mother said you weren't back yet. I just wanted to make sure you were okay, you know, nothing wrong from the other night."

I kissed Noah on the cheek. "I'm fine, I'm just catching up on my sleep."

He smiled as I looked down. An awkward pause had him rubbing the back of his neck.

"Oh okay, well I'll let you sleep then. Just give me a call tomorrow. Maybe we can do something."

"Yeah, maybe," I said, slowly sinking behind the door. "Bye."

Noah flashed his hand, and I shut the door, letting out a long sigh. I watched him through the blinds as he walked up the steps and looked back. Then he was in his truck and on his way.

I looked down at Lily, who was standing at my feet. "I'm romantic, huh?"

—◦◦◦—

Monday morning I didn't wake up early, didn't go to the café, and I did not go to Georgia Harvest's house as I was accustomed. Instead I took the liberty of going through all the clothes I had and selling them to a local store. Then I took the money I made from that just outside of Franklin to the nearest mall. I decided it was time for a new, sophisticated wardrobe change.

Cassie came along with me. She was attending a fashion school in the fall. I figured she'd know what she was talking about. I was having a great time. I bought several blouses, jeans, skirts, and dresses and a few pair of heels, which was a rarity. I got my hair cut to just above my shoulders, and I dyed it to a light chestnut color. I really began to believe in the saying, "You look good, you feel good!"

Cassie and I made our way to the food court around three. We both ordered veggie pizza and sat in the middle of the court.

"Why did you move to New York?"

Cassie asked the question I felt I had answered more than enough before. "I wanted to be a writer, and working part time at the small paper in Franklin just wasn't enough for me, so when I thought I had saved up enough money—which, boy, was I wrong—I moved to the big city thinking that so many papers would want me that I'd get to pick and choose."

I took a sip of my coke. "Well, I got an apartment, which I couldn't afford, and ended up working a job, which I despised. Nothing ever came out of it, so as you know, I moved back here, and now I'm just slowly trying to find projects to work on and keep myself sane."

Cassie smiled. "I bet you hate being back here. I can't wait to leave this place. There's nothing here worth staying. I'm glad there's someone else who thinks so too."

I raised my brow. "I didn't say I hated it here, and what about my brother? Isn't he worth staying for?"

Cassie was quick to speak. "No." She looked up, seeing I was offended. "I mean Bryan's a great guy, and we're having our fun now, but I mean he wants to stay here, and this town is too small for me so, no. I mean, he knows we're just having fun." She picked up her pizza and took a bite, nodding and smiling as if I agreed.

"Does he know that?" I remarked.

She looked down at her phone for the time and said, "We should probably head back."

The ride back was saved by the radio. When I pulled into the driveway Cassie got out in a flash and ran to hug my brother.

"You two have fun today?" Bryan said, smiling with Cassie around his neck.

I shook my head yes and kept moving. As soon as I got into the house, my mother gave me a countdown to dinner, and my father urged me to come watch how vultures clean up the highways. I looked up to see a large bird picking at an unidentifiable creature.

"No, thanks, I'll pass."

My father asked if I was sure.

"Rain check, Dad."

I went down to my bedroom, opening the bags of clothes and shoes and pulling out all the empty hangers in the back closet and organizing everything. When I had finished, my phone rang. It was Noah.

"Meaghan." My mother knocked on the door. "Dinner is served!"

I forwarded the call and went upstairs. My mother had made stuffed pork chops, mashed potatoes, and steamed broccoli. I was silent most of the conversation. I spoke about my hair color, which my mother adored and my father despised. There was a small debate between them about the color. I looked over to see Cassie whispering in my brother's ears and him smiling, totally oblivious to what was actually happening, and twice more my phone vibrated, Noah. I felt as if the room were spinning. I stood, sliding the chair across the tile, making everyone look up. I cleared my plate and went back downstairs.

A whole week went by. I hadn't been to Georgia's, I hadn't seen Noah, and I avoided going into town for fear I might bump in to him and have to explain myself. I remember in high school a teacher had said, "Secrets are dangerous, poisonous thorns." I slowly was beginning to understand that. I was hiding from Georgia, from Noah, from Bryan, from myself. Then I came to the realization while watching I Love Lucy that if I wasn't being real with anyone, I at least had to be real with myself.

I bought a paper and searched for any local writing jobs. The closest thing I found was a thirteen-year-old boy who was in need of a creative writing tutor.

I looked down at Lily, who was licking her paws. "That doesn't sound too bad."

Her head tilted to the side.

"You're right, it sounds horrible."

I needed the money and couldn't find any other opportunities, so I decided the pay was decent enough to help this kid out for a few weeks. I called up a Mrs. Shepherd and had an interview with her the next morning. The home was a small beautiful home, built of gray brick, giving it a cottage effect. I knocked only once and was greeted by a tall brunette with small circle glasses and a pout lip. She looked to be in her early fifties.

"Hi, you must be Meaghan."

I shook my head yes, taken aback by her high-pitched voice.

"I'm Mrs. Shepherd. You can call me Kathy. I'm Jake's mother. He's in his bedroom, Come in and I'll give you a tour and talk some things over with you."

I followed Kathy to her kitchen, which was a bright yellow. She asked me to please sit and offered me some sweet tea, which I didn't dare resist.

When she sat, she had her long bony finger gripped around her cup and smiled. "So have you tutored before?"

"No, I haven't, but I am a writer. I used to write for the Franklin paper in high school and I'm currently working on a bit of a story."

"Oh impressive, I always admired people who could write." She lifted the glass mug to her red lips. "I never had the talent, and either does my son Jake. He's thirteen, and he is doing great in all his classes with the exception of writing, I decided after his teacher's recommendation to find him a tutor. Now he's a boy, mind you, and a teen." She pulled her glasses off, wiping the circle lenses. "He can be quite troublesome often."

"Listen, Kathy, I'm not great with kids. I'm not sure what I'm even doing here to be honest. I just needed something to take my mind off of things and a few dollars in my pocket."

"I would pay you ten dollars every hour you spend with him. He has a few big papers coming up, and I need him to pass. You're the only person who has responded. Please at least meet him." She looked so desperate for help. Even if I didn't like him, the money wasn't bad.

"All right, I'll meet him."

I opened the door to a short, chubby boy who had freckles like the sky has stars. He was sitting at a wooden desk with his back facing the door.

As soon as I entered, he turned, looking at his mother. "Who's the babe?" he asked smiling.

His mother scolded him and apologized to me. I noticed he had chocolate smeared across his cheek.

"Hi, Jake," I said after his mother went on with the introductions.

"Look," he began, "I'm the man of the house. I don't need a babysitter,"

"Well, I'm a tutor, so I won't be babysitting you at all."

He stood and wobbled over to me, putting his arm on the doorframe and his hand on his hip. He had a creepy little smirk on his face. "Well in that case, tutor me all you want, baby."

Again his mother scolded him, and she walked me out to my car. "So then, can you start tomorrow?"

"Yeah, tomorrow."

I drove back into the center of town, feeling purposeless again.

Chapter 10

I met a hyper Mrs. Shepherd at the door around three in the afternoon. She had tea waiting for me at the kitchen table, and Jake was sitting there surrounded by loose-leaf paper, pencils, and a blue sharpener, and he was currently working on a microwavable burrito.

"Now I have all the supplies he could possibly need. I'll be gone for an hour, and Jake has promised he will behave." Kathy had her hands crossed and was looking sternly at Jake.

"I know, Mom. Everything's under control. You can leave now." Jake shook his head at his mother and went in for another bite.

"Meaghan, you have all privilege to discipline within your means. You're in charge, and I'll see you at 4:15 sharp. Thank you again."

I sighed as she shut the door. I looked at my watch and then over to Jake, who had dropped melted cheese and meat on his blue shirt. He saw it was too far down to lick off, so he just let it lay there.

"Okay, Jake, your mom says you have a few big papers coming up, so can I see the criteria your teacher has set for the first paper?"

Jake started pushing through papers on the table, managing to get grease on each one. He handed me a white list. I grabbed it from the only clean corner, reading over each line.

"Okay, so you have to create your own fairy tale. It shouldn't be that hard. You seem like a pretty imaginative kid."

Jake smiled, licking his fingers. "I am, baby."

"Look, Jake, you can call me Meaghan, and that's all you may call me. I'm going out on a whim to help you. You need my help, not the other way around, so are we going to work together to get your mom off your back, or will this be my last day with you?" I looked at him sternly as I had seen his mother do.

"Okay, Meaghan, I'm sorry. So how do we start this thing?"

Kathy had arrived at 4:15 as promised. She practically ran in the door in shock that I had stuck around. She thanked me again for my time again, and I was on my way back home for the day. I drove through the town center and saw Noah's truck parked in front of the café. He must have been treating himself to some black coffee and apple churros for his mother. As I sat at the red light I saw him coming out the door. He looked tired and had his shirt un-tucked and his boot-laces swinging freely about. The red charger behind me honked. The light had turned green, and I saw Noah's eyes in my mirror as I hit the gas forward.

I wanted to call him and ask if everything was all right. I wasn't sure if he looked so worn because of Georgia or because of me, but then I shook my head. If Georgia broke the news to him, he would be at my house in a rage. It must have been over me then, and as much as I wanted to console him, I didn't dare call him that whole day or the next.

I had been going to Jake's three days in a row now. We finished his first paper today and turned it in. I had spent three hours the second day and two today. We were getting along well. His attempts to hit on me were less frequent, and I began not minding spending time with him. His mother had told me after today's session that she was very thankful for me. She said Jake had had four other tutors who all left after the first or second day.

"You've really taught him to step his game up. Oh, the movers are here!" Kathy said, cutting her sentence short.

I looked out the window in surprise to see my fathers' moving van and Noah sitting in the passenger seat. "No way," I whispered.

"What?" Kathy said, puzzled.

"Oh, what are you getting shipped here today?" I said, stuttering, trying to make a recovery.

"I bought a table for the living room. The old one was just too outdated."

I watched Noah lifting the opposite of my father. I told Kathy I had to use the restroom and walked down the hall and shut the door just as I heard Noah ask where she wanted it. As Noah read off the bill, I heard my father ask if he could use the restroom. My heart was pounding, and I just sat frozen on the side of the tub. My father knocked, and I opened the door, pulling him in.

"Meaghan!"

"Shhhh, Dad! Please don't blow my cover!" I looked at him sympathetically.

"What are you doing here? And why are you hiding in the bathroom?" My father looked very angry.

"Dad, listen, I'll explain everything at home. Please don't tell Noah I'm here. Just don't mention anything about me."

"I want a full explanation when I get home, which is after this delivery. I expect you to be there, and as far as not saying anything, don't worry. I won't blow your cover."

I hugged my dad as he walked out of the bathroom, and I made my way into the kitchen. As my father's moving van pulled away, I grabbed my messenger bag, said good-bye to the Shepherds, and made my way home.

My father was polishing the wood on the pool tables in the basement. I sat on my futon, and he continued to polish.

He stood up, pulling the gray cover across and throwing the rag down. "What's going on Meaghan?"

"I'm working on a project, and I've become emotionally attached like I told you the other night, but I feel it's best if I just avoid the whole thing, so I stopped working the project entirely, which means avoiding every person involved in the project, which includes Noah."

My father stared at me. I could tell he didn't understand. "I thought you liked Noah, and honestly he's been under the weather lately because you haven't been talking to him."

"I know, Dad. I really like him, but it's so complicated."

"Well, life's complicated, Meaghan, and I didn't raise you to only face what you wanted to. You have to stand up and face everything around you, every obstacle, every maze. You can't beat around the bush with life. You need to talk to him."

"I know, Dad. I just don't know how to start."

My father walked over and kissed my forehead. "You're the writer. You always know how to start." He walked up the stairs and left me in my room.

I drove over to Georgia's after a short day with Jake. I left him with his mother eating pizza rolls and playing Grand Theft Auto. I was surprised to see Georgia sitting on her white wicker chair on the porch. I had never seen her outside. She had her yellow pitcher of tea siting on the matching wicker stand and raised her hand up, blocking the sun to see me.

"Meaghan? Is that you dear?" I wasn't expecting such a warm response, but I was glad she started the conversation.

"Yeah, it's me."

I walked up on the porch, setting my messenger bag on the chair beside her. The wicker stand with the yellow pitcher stood in between us. Georgia had a hardback copy of the Pride and the Prejudice sitting on her lap.

She noticed my interest and said, "I heard it was a good read. I figured now would be as good a time as any to read it." Georgia smiled.

She looked frail, maybe ten pounds lighter than the last time I saw her. Her hair was short. I could tell she had it cut in hopes of disguising her hair loss. It would buy her a little more time to explain to Noah. She looked worn and tired. Her eyes were heavy as if she had not rested in days.

Georgia offered me some tea, and while she was pouring my glass as she insisted, tears slowly came to my eyes as I watched her struggle with two hands to lift the pitcher. I was quick to grab the glass from her, and I tried to hold back my emotions as much as possible.

"So what have you been up too this whole, oh, what has it been, three weeks now?"

I sat down my glass. "I picked up a part-time tutoring job. This boy, his name is Jake, he needs help with creative writing, and the pay isn't bad. Other than that, nothing much more. Spent some quality time with my family, thought some things over. What about you, Georgia? What have you been up to?"

Georgia smirked. "I've made a few changes. I cut my hair shorter, if you hadn't noticed." She played with it freely.

"I did, it suits you well," I said, quick to gulp more tea.

"Thank you, and well, I've been reading this book. It's lovely, and I spent some time in my garden growing a few things here and there, spent some time with my boy." Georgia looked up at me, and I looked down at my sneakers, avoiding the subject entirely. "What made you come back up here today?" Georgia asked with a glimmer in her eyes.

"Well, I have a project to do, and I missed you and the sweet tea and the turkey sandwiches every day, and I came back here today hoping you'd allow me to come back and finish my project." I looked at Georgia with an earnest face. I had truly been longing to hear the rest of the story.

"Of course, I'd be honored to have you back, and I did miss you a whole lot, girl. Come on over here."

I stood and hugged Georgia. The tears I managed to hide earlier were now sliding down my cheeks. She felt so fragile in my arms, much different than the solid woman I had met a while ago.

Georgia pulled back. "All right, enough of that. Let's head on into the kitchen and get this tour bus back on the road."

"How's Noah been?" I managed to squeak out as we sat at the table.

Georgia shook her head. "He hasn't been the same happy camper as when you were around every day, but he's a strong boy. He's really just been working a lot, picking up extra hours, saving his money up for whatever next big project he's working on, but I know it would just make the difference if you stayed for dinner, talked to him a bit." Georgia had a sort of glimmer in her eyes.

"Yeah, we'll see. I just want to focus on our big project at the moment."

Georgia shook her head in agreement. "All right you remember where we left off?"

"The woman, Cynthia, she was hit," I said quickly.

"Ah yes," Georgia said. "So I had stayed at Loretta's for two days by myself. Her and John refused to let me go, saying there was still a scene out front and too many reporters lingering. They didn't want anyone coming in and hounding me with questions, having me recite the whole incident. I agreed, because I was still very shaken up, but I also felt they didn't want me around the reporters for fear I might mention her being in the store hysterical, and from what I heard my uncle saying in private the other night, the police had stopped by their store, saying that a customer had said Cynthia came into the store in hysterical. My aunt had said only that she was a difficult customer, complaining about a piece of jewelry she had purchased. She wanted to return it, but it was past the thirty-day return policy, so she stormed out in a fit, and that's when, well, the incident occurred.

"I was so shocked at my aunt's story, and even more shocked when I heard my uncle tell her that was great improvising that should keep the hounds away. I felt I could not trust them to a certain extent. This was a woman's life, and they lied to the authorities. I wondered if something had happened to me if they would do the same to hide whatever it was they felt the need to keep secret."

"Why didn't you just go to the police and tell them everything?" I questioned.

Georgia shook her head. "I had thought of that one night. Then I sat right back down on the bed my relatives had provided me with, eating the food they had provided me with, wearing one of the dresses they had provided me with. I had a good roof over my head. I was earning a decent wage, and it was all because of my aunt and uncle. If I had explained to the police what really happened, there was a great chance that they would keep them in custody, and if they linked what happened to Billy with Cynthia's death, they would imprison them for sure. I had nowhere to go and hardly enough saved up to get me anywhere."

"It was a Friday, and my uncle was out of town doing business. My Aunt Loretta had a large shipment of jewelry coming in, and she said she would need my help cashiering and doing inventory.

"'It's impossible to do it all by my lonesome, and most of the crowd has cleared in front of the store. Will you come on down with me and help your aunty out?' my aunt said, her red lips revealing a white smile.

"'Sure, I've missed the store a little.'

"My aunt opened the door and quickly urged me inside as she watched my eyes fixed on the yellow caution tape shaking in the light breeze we had that day.

"'Okay,' she said, locking the door as she always did so we could prepare the store before the customers entered. 'Here's the money for the register. Count it, mark it down, oh, you know the routine. My shipment will be here around twelve, so we'll have to clear the back room a little, bring out more displays, and set them up. We've got a lot of work to do.'

"I pulled the ivory sheet off the counter we used to keep the dust off. I sat all the displays from the back into the glass shelves, which encompassed the register. I was counting the money when I heard my aunt walking up the stairs. She hadn't pulled the curtain down, so I tiptoed backward until my back hit the shelf. I stretched to see the whole way to the top of the stairs. A small window stood at the top of the steps. I heard her making her way across the banister to come back down and jumped back over to the register drawer, putting all the money away. I watched her drop the curtain and dust off her hands.

"'Okay, darling, flip the sign, and we are open for business!'

"It was closer to the holiday. Thanksgiving was the next day and, the store was the busiest I had ever seen. I was waiting for a lady to count out her change. I took a glimpse at the line I still had to get through. My aunt was so busy setting out displays. She would set up one and come out with another, just to see the one she had just set up was almost empty! A lot of the women in line were older and spent their time gossiping about the latest.

"I heard one woman who wore a long blue dress trimmed in white speak about Cynthia. 'You've read the papers about her husband? He's still knocked. He doesn't know she's dead yet. How horrible it will be when he wakes up. I was thinking about sending over some baked goods.'

"The other women agreed.

"Then one large woman wearing a black skirt said, "I heard he had her killed. Everyone knows he had his fingers dipped in mafia deeds.'

"The other women gasped, and the chatter filled the room. I raised my head at the gossip. I looked over to my aunt, who was just helping a customer.

"She looked enraged at the conversation, and with all the elegance in the world, she stood in front of the line. 'Now, ladies, what happened was a tragedy. Need we disrespect the dead with gossip? For now only, 5 percent off all merchandise.'

"The ladies cheered and thanked my aunt like she was a celebrity. I saw the power beaming off of her. I was quieter now, just ringing up customers like a robot until I got to the end of the line. It was four thirty, and my aunt announced we'd be closing at five. I moved slowly. I was so focused on the gossip. I remembered my mother saying once that gossip was partial truth.

"'I'm too tired to even fathom up a meal,' my aunt said, lighting a cigarette. 'Let's go out for some dinner.'

"I followed her out the door and into the car.

"'Here.' She handed me a white envelope.

"'What is it?' I said.

"'It's for your hard work today. I couldn't have handled that crowd without you. Just think of it as a Thanksgiving bonus.'

"My aunt smiled as I opened the envelope. There was a small bundle of bills.

"'Thank you, Aunt Loretta!'

"I hadn't had that much money in my hands ever. My mood quickly changed as we drove down the strip. I saw a sign that read 'Billy's Deli.' The lights were black, and yellow tape hugged the building. I looked down at the money and wondered if it came from the business we had today or from what went on behind the red curtain."

Chapter 11

I stood to crack the windows. It was getting warmer in the kitchen. Georgia offered more tea. I shook my head no. I was waiting for the next sentence.

"Three years had passed. Not much had happened, but for a short summary, Bill never came out of the hospital. The doctors had revealed to him his wife's untimely death, and his condition only worsened afterward. The store stayed busy through the holidays and slowed down some the rest of the year. I had saved up plenty of money to be on my way, but it hadn't occurred to me to leave until my aunt asked me one evening. We were sitting in a small diner we often stopped by after work.

"'What's your next move, Georgia?' She let out a swirl of smoke.

"'What do you mean?' I asked, sipping my chocolate shake.

"'I mean, I was thinking about you this morning. I ran into a gentleman at the pumps, and I heard him talking. He was saying him and his wife had packed up all their belongings and decided to travel all the states, or until they fell in love with one place. Then they would settle there.' She exhaled once more. 'I got to thinking then about you, like I said. How set you were on traveling when I first saw you. And, well, it's been some time. I just wondered if you were done or if this is where you wanted to settle.'

"I stared at my aunt, and she quickly spoke up. 'I'm not telling you to leave. Lord knows you can stay with us until the end of time. I was just wondering, is all, what your next step was. Do you even have any idea?'

"I didn't say much on the way home. I took a bath that night and lay in my room with the lights off for some time, just thinking. What was my next move? It drove me crazy all night. I flipped the light switch in the early morning, searching for my uncle's map. I decided to close my eyes and just go wherever my finger landed. New Jersey? I couldn't believe it, really. I would literally be going from one coast to the other. I had never been very far east, and then I began thinking I didn't know anyone else. I've stretched my contacts already.

"My aunt called for me. I slipped my shoes on, and we headed for the store. It was a hot afternoon in the middle of August. I brought up the conversation with my aunt about Jersey.

"'New Jersey, why that's on the whole other side. That's quite a trip!' my uncle said. I could tell he was utterly against it.

"My aunt, however, said, 'That sounds like quite the adventure, Georgia. I don't know how you'll get over there, but John's older sister Sophia lives in New Jersey. She's a kind spirit. She'd love for you to stay, I know it. Right, John?' My aunt looked over to my uncle, who had his hand on the back of his neck.

"'Well, yeah, she wouldn't mind company. She's always complaining she hasn't any. I just don't like the idea of you leaving by yourself.'

"I stood with my arm on the register. 'I wouldn't be leaving right away. It could be days, or months, maybe even another year. I'd be fine. I've been on the road before. Did you really think I was going to stay forever?'

"My uncle and aunt laughed. 'We had hoped!' they said in unison.

"My birthday was a few weeks later. My aunt and uncle had left the store. I was alone. We hadn't been busy lately, so I sat on the metal chair behind the register booth. I stared at the curtain and stared at the clock and then back at the curtain. I walked over to the front door. I locked it and flipped the 'We'll be right back' sign. I ran over to the curtain and lifted it just so I could go under. It was a heavier material than I had guessed.

"I stood at the base of fifteen gray, worn steps. The small window I had once seen peeking through the side of the curtain shone brightly. It looked as if the sun was situated in that room. I could feel the intense heat as I climbed the stairs. When I got to the top, I could see over the banister a wooden table with five chairs around it. Nothing else was up there but the chairs and the table. I bolted back down the stairs to get back to my post and escape the unbearable heat. I realized I couldn't have spared one more second up there, because when I went to the door to flip the sign back, I saw my aunt and uncle pulling up. I turned the lock and ran back behind the register.

"'Hello, birthday girl,' my uncle said. I could see he was hiding something behind his back.

"My aunt followed behind him, flipping the closed sign. 'We're going home. I got dinner and a cake for you, and John, show her what you got,' my aunt urged him.

"'Here she is!' He pulled a small black kitten from around his back.

"I ran to it. I had never had a pet before. 'Oh she's darling!' I said in excitement.

"'Isn't she?' my aunt said. 'We got her from the rescue agency. Her name is Baby, but you're welcome to change it if you like.'

"'No,' I said, holding her close. 'Baby suits her fine.'

Georgia smiled. "I took that cat everywhere with me. She was my partner in crime. It's a nice thing to have someone to talk to, someone you can just rattle off anything too and they won't judge you or throw in their opinion."

I nodded my head in agreement.

"Well Noah will be home in about twenty minutes. I'm going to start dinner. Why don't you stay, Meaghan? Really, what's the worst that could happen?" Georgia smiled.

"He could come in and cut my head off." I laughed. "I'll stay, but the moment I'm not welcome, I'll leave you two."

I was nervous about staying from the get-go, but it was hard to deny Georgia's smiling pleas, especially after we had just reconciled. I was standing by the fridge when Noah walked in. I saw him look down at his dirty clothes and Georgia motion him upstairs to change.

When he came back down, he said, "Meaghan, I didn't know you'd be here. How have you been?"

"Fine," I said, setting the pitcher of cold tea on the table and moving toward Georgia, who was mashing the potatoes. "I picked up a tutoring job, so I won't be around as much as before."

Noah sat at the table. "That's nice, I never knew you to be a tutor. I'm sure you're good at it." Noah opened a beer nervously.

Georgia made most of the conversation at the table. After dinner, I walked to my car with Noah following behind me. He grabbed and kissed me. I felt dazed as if any movement I would lose my footing and fall.

"Noah, I'm…I've been gone… I'm just trying to figure some things out."

"It's fine, just please don't disappear again. I thought I hurt you or something."

I let go of his hand and got in the driver's seat. "I'm the only one that's done any hurting," I said as I waved goodnight.

I took a picture of Jake eating his hot pockets while writing his essay. I had lost count of days in my challenge, so now they were marked as "Georgia Harvest Challenge: Days Lost." I would go to Jake's for half the day and then to Georgia's. When I got home at night I was exhausted. I would wake up happy, though, because I had something to do every day, and it was something I enjoyed doing every day.

I told Jake one afternoon to make sure, despite his mother's opinion or his father's or anyone else's, to do what he wanted to when he got out of high school. I told him to promise me he'd do whatever he wanted, become who he wanted to be. I began to feel the sense of freedom and happiness Georgia had described to me at the beginning of her journey.

Noah met me at the café later that evening. We shared a chocolate mousse cheesecake. I had tea, and he had a black coffee.

"You like tutoring that kid?"

"Yeah, I mean, it's not too bad. He's a good kid, and the pay isn't anything to complain about. This is my last week with him." I slid my fork across the plate, dragging another small piece of cake toward me.

"I've been real happy seeing you lately. I mean, more often than never." Noah smiled.

"Yeah, I like seeing you too." I lifted the tea bag out of my cup, dropping it on the floral napkin.

"I like you a lot, Meaghan. I wanted to tell you I consider you my girl, I just wanted to know if it was a mutual understanding."

I smiled, putting down my fork and reaching my hand over to Noah's. "Yeah, I'm your girl, Noah."

Sometime after our cheesecake was gone and our drinks were empty, Noah walked me to my car and kissed me goodnight. As I shut my door, he tapped on the window. I rolled it down.

"Yeah?" I said, smiling.

"Come home with me. Just spend the night."

I laughed. "I've got to tutor tomorrow. I'll just stick to my futon."

He walked away and then ran back. "Just come stay with me."

I couldn't deny the sweet look in his eyes. "Okay, I'll follow you."

I never felt a deeper connection with another man in my life. I felt so safe in his arms. He spoke in a soft whisper, sending chills down my back. I was in love with Noah Harvest. I didn't want anyone else. I wished the feeling I had that night would never escape my body, my mind, and especially my heart.

Chapter 12

"It was the day before I had decided to head out to New Jersey. I had been conversing with my Uncle John's sister, Sophia, and she seemed more excited to have me as a guest than I was to travel. The days leading up to my sudden trip were strange. In a summary my aunt had received letters in yellow envelopes sticking in the door handle of the store. From the first letter she had received, I could tell something was wrong just by the frightened expression on her face.

"She was much quieter in those days, and when she had shown my uncle those letters, he was in an angry fit. I hadn't got to read any of them. My aunt was careful never to let them lie around, and she hadn't spoken about them to me. My uncle told me one evening that he wanted me to leave within the following days, and until I left I was to stay close to them. His voice was stern. I didn't dare question him.

"Every day the letters continued, and every day my uncle's warnings sounded more and more worried. One day—it was around noon—my aunt had been upstairs behind the red curtain for hours.

"She came down the stairs, wiping sweat from her forehead. 'Come on. I've got to make a stop. Clear the register and flip the sign.'

We had never closed mid-day. I was beyond curious and did as directed by my aunt. She was already in the car when I locked the door. In minutes we were in front of the familiar cigar shop I had seen when I first arrived in Vegas.

"My aunt looked at the two large men outside, who I assumed were guards of some sort, and then turned to me. 'Stay in the car no matter what. If I'm not out in twenty minutes or if anyone comes over to the car, turn it on and haul it back home, okay?'

"I shook my head in confusion. My aunt walked in, and the two guards followed behind her. I noticed my aunt walk through a red velvet curtain similar to the one in the jewelry store. I figured now that it had been a symbol for something, as I had noticed one in the clothing store my aunt had taken me my second day here.

"When twenty minutes passed, I noticed there was no one in the front of the store, so I allowed my curiosity to get to me. I opened the front door and went it. It smelt of smoke and alcohol. As soon as I went in I heard voices in the back. The curtain was down. I couldn't see anyone, but I heard a great deal.

"A fast-talking man said, 'Lo, we were partners, you and John and I. I thought I could trust you twos with anything.'

"My aunt spoke but was interrupted.

"'So here I am reading the paper. These detectives are bringing up some case about a deli worker and his wife. Now I thought I killed them a long time ago, and I also thought that you twos took care of it. You know the rules, Lo. You do dirty work, you don't let a stain!' I heard him slam a paper down. 'This is a huge stain!'

"I heard a chair slide back and my aunt speak up. 'Jackson, this is not John's or my fault. It is not our responsibility. We left no traces of anything. If anything came up, it would be from Tony's sloppy job with Cynthia. There was a crowd of people then and blood and tire marks. Jesus, you can still see the tire marks. As far as the deli goes, there is nothing there, nothing. I can put a guarantee on my work, and you know that.'

"There was silence. I covered my mouth in shock. My aunt and uncle had killed a man.

"'Lo, listen to me. You got the letters. You know the man power I have. If you or John or even that little niece of yours gets in the way of anything I'm doing, I'm going to take you out. You know how I operate. This is a business. Just stay clear of me and don't come in here unless I call you, understand?'

"'Yeah, I understand.'

"I bolted out of the store and sat in the car with a blank expression like I had been sitting there the whole time. My heart was pounding as my aunt walked out. The two guards returned to their positions. I closed my eyes and took a deep breath in attempt to slow my heart rate down.

"My aunt pulled the door open and sat down. 'I thought I told you to leave after twenty minutes.' She smiled.

"'I wasn't paying mind to the time,' I said, expressionless.

"I didn't see her as the same woman. I was ready to go back to the house and pack. I had planned to leave. Sophia and my Aunt Loretta had arranged a flight for me. I was so nervous to fly. It would be my first time, but I agreed to it. I didn't want to take my chances hitchhiking again.

"My aunt and uncle had taken me to the airport two days later. They even paid for Baby to come with me. Saying good-bye wasn't hard for me. I saw them for what they were. I felt a sort of fear toward them now. The ride to the airport wasn't filled with much conversation on my part. My uncle John did most of the talking, telling me stories of his sister. I noticed my aunt looking at me in the mirror. My eyes met hers twice. I felt like she knew I had heard everything, but she was erasing it in her mind, telling herself it was impossible for me to know, because I was in the car the whole time, but I could tell the thought still lingered in her mind.

"Minutes before I boarded my aunt leaned over and hugged me tightly. 'I want to explain everything, Georgia, so you don't have the wrong idea.'

"I sat on the metal bench. My ears were perked.

"'Jackson is the man who owns the cigar shop. He is mafia related. I work for him, your uncle too.' She was staring at me, concerned. 'We had nothing. We had hit rock bottom with the store. Jackson came in one day and offered us a deal, saying if we partnered with him our business would only flourish. The way he spoke and the money he flashed was too enticing to refuse.

"'Everything was incredible at first. The store was just a front, like some of the other stores on the block. He came in, put a red curtain in our shop, which was a sign of affiliation. We would simply collect money from others. They brought it to us, and we took it to Jackson.

"'Then things started getting bad, and fast. Your uncle was gone long one night. I was worried sick. He came home late at night, shaking. Jackson had demanded him to shoot a man who owed him money. John said if he didn't Jackson was going to ruin us. He had no choice. After the first knockoff more jobs of the sort came to us. Jackson had always had us at the balls. It was never a partnership, but we were in too deep then to get out. You can only imagine how deep we are now.' My aunt stared at me, hoping I understood.

"'Why don't you just get up and move then?'

"'Jackson is one hell of a guy. You cross him and he'll kill you. There's nowhere in this world we'd be safe. That's why the next knockoff we have planned is Jackson's. Then we'd be free, and so would all the others who wear the burden of the red curtain.'

"My flight was called. I stood and hugged my aunt. 'I don't understand at all. You have to see what you are doing is wrong. Please be careful, and thank you for everything, Loretta. I will keep in touch.'

"She touched my shoulder and wiped a tear from her cheek. 'It's best if you don't. John and I will contact you when it's safe. I never intended on you being involved in all this chaos. I'm trying to keep it that way.'

"I started walking away, and she called for me once more. 'Georgia, you were in the shop, weren't you? You heard everything?'

"I shook my head yes.

"She laughed. 'I should have known better. You have your mother's curiosity.'

"I don't remember much of the flight. I hadn't slept well for days, as you could imagine, so when I hit that seat, I fell asleep. I had sat beside a lovely blonde woman. She reminded me somewhat of Candice who

I had hitchhiked with long before. She woke me as we landed.

"'Darling, we've landed. You best wake up now," she said in a soothing country accent.

"I only had a description from my uncle of Sophia. She had long black hair and bright green eyes, and she was around five foot three or so with a beautiful smile. As I stepped into the main lobby as we had agreed, I heard someone yelling my name. I turned to my right to see Sophia shaking a white sign that read, 'Georgia!' in blue marker.

"'Sophia?' I said as she put the sign under her arm and hugged me.

"'Yes! Oh you look exactly how Loretta described you.'

"I smiled. 'Yes, you fit your description well also.'

"She grabbed my green suitcase while I carried my leather brown bag.

"'Well I'm very excited to have you. I've got a house and no one to share anything with. I haven't had company in years. It'll be wonderful having a girl staying around. We can go out and just have loads of fun!'

"I walked where the animals were held and found Baby purring as I picked up her cage. Sophia showed us the way to her van, and we only had a short drive before arriving at her home. The house was the biggest I had ever been in. We pulled into a white stone driveway, and she parked her van under a gray roofed carport. I followed her up the white steps, holding on to the black banister. There were four white rocking chairs on the porch, a small table in between each, and yellow tulips in tall vases on those tables.

"'This was my grandmother's home. She passed it on to me since I was the only one in the family who stuck around.'

"She opened the screen door, introducing the wooden flooring in the foyer. To the left was the living room and to the right the dining room. Straight ahead were thirty steps to the second floor embellished with a sleek black banister snaking around the whole floor, hinting to a Victorian design.

"'My grandfather had worked very hard on this place, my grandmother too. They told me that when they first moved in it was just a rubble building. They constructed all this.'

"Sophia showed me the kitchen, which was breathtaking. In the back a tall white door gave view to the very lush, green garden out back. The sun shone through the three large windows opposite the stove, lighting up the whole kitchen. A long eat-in bar topped with gray speckled marble ran the length of the sink. On the other side of it two large vases, like the ones on the porch, were filled with more tulips.

"'I usually eat here at the bar. I can't fathom the last time I sat in the dining room. My grandparents used to host card games out there. They always had company.' Sophia grabbed grapes from the fridge. 'Me, on the other hand, not so much.'

"We walked up the stairs. Sophia showed me the small library just at the top of the stairs. She welcomed me to read all the books I wanted. Just down the hall was a bathroom, and at the very end was my room. It was lovely, painted a deep purple with lily murals on the accent wall. A tall, slender bookcase stood beside the queen bed covered with a bright orange comforter.

"'Do you like it?' Sophia questioned, eating her grapes.

"'Oh, yes, it's a fine room. Can I let Baby out?'

"Sophia smiled. 'Let her roam free. She's a good cat. I've been watching her.'

"I opened Baby's cage, and she jumped straight on to my bed. Sophia left and let me unpack. I was so happy to be in such a beautiful home. I pulled out my silver box with all my pictures in it from my trip. I sat looking at all of them as I often did. I was in awe of all the interesting people I had met so far and all the lessons I had learned from all of them. I was wondering now where my travels would end."

Georgia stopped talking as soon as she heard Noah's truck. I was quick to put away my notebook.

He walked in carrying two roses. "Here's two roses for my two ladies."

Georgia and I laughed.

"How sweet, Noah." Georgia kissed his cheek and moaned in pain.

"Mom, you all right?" Noah said, concerned.

I looked worriedly at Georgia, who was shooing him away. "I'm fine, just sore today is all." Georgia laughed awkwardly as if to shake everything off.

I continued to stare at her, and for a moment I could have sworn I saw doubt in Noah's eyes, like he already knew his mother's illness, but he couldn't have. I shook my head at the thought.

"Well, I better get home. I have Jake's paper to edit, and I've got to go meet up with him in the morning, plus I've got my other things to edit, so Georgia, I'll see you tomorrow. Noah, you want to walk me out?"

"Yeah, of course."

Noah held the door for me, and we walked out on to the driveway. I pulled my leather jacket tight. The fall breeze had already begun creeping out at night, making us all aware that it was just around the corner. The sky was dark, and the stars bright.

"It's beautiful out tonight, isn't it?" I said, turning to Noah, who was admiring the sky.

"Yeah, I always liked this time of year around here. It's still warm enough to sit out, and the breeze keeps you from sweating."

I hopped in my jeep, leaving the door slightly ajar. Noah stood with my legs wrapped around him and kissed my forehead.

"I want to go out this Friday. Let's go to the movies or something. I just want to spend some time with you. I feel like when I get home you're always leaving, and when I leave for work in the morning, you're just getting here. I hate only see you for ten or fifteen minutes a day." Noah held me tightly.

"I've been busy with Jake and other things. I just haven't had the time. I should be free Friday, though. A movie sounds perfect. I can't remember the last time I've seen one."

Noah smiled. "Friday it is then, and what's this project you say you're working on? I'd like to hear about it."

I looked up, pushing his hair back and kissing him. "I'll see you tomorrow, goodnight." I backed out of the driveway, feeling more guilty than anything.

The next two days I hadn't done much. Georgia spoke about Sophia's home and gardening and such, small details I would add to fill the lines of the story. I had only seen Noah for a few minutes each day as usual, and Jake's mother cancelled, because Jake, who just started school again, came down with a bad cough.

It was Friday evening before anything productive had really happened; Noah had called me to let me know he'd be picking me up around 7:30, so I showered and got dressed and met him at my door at 7:30 sharp.

"Where are we going?" I asked, climbing into the passenger seat.

"Just to Pete's for a few slices, then to the movies. That all right with you, boss?" Noah asked, smiling.

"Yes, it'll do, peasant."

We laughed. When we got into Pete's it was busy as expected for a Friday night. We sat in the same booth as on our first date. Noah had loads to talk about, and I didn't say much, as I was thinking. It's such a burden to put your thoughts on hold. I wanted to tell him how honored I was to be writing his mother's story. I wanted to tell him all her journeys and the people she was meeting and how much this project was impacting my life, but I couldn't speak on it, so the conversation was always very dry on my part.

Noah took me to see a scary movie. While others around me were jumping and holding their date tightly, I was too focused on not bringing my thoughts up that I sat there in a daze. Twice Noah tried to pull me close, and I pushed away. If I hadn't ruined the night so far, when he drove me home I kissed him on the cheek and walked to my door. I saw his car idling there for a few moments after I was inside. He was probably wondering what the hell happened.

I slunk over to my futon, like the Grinch who stole Christmas slithered around the Christmas tree stealing the presents. I kicked off my shoes and lay there with Lily at my ear. I was quick to fall asleep that night, hoping my dreams would allow me to escape reality until morning.

Chapter 13

I saw Jake at eleven the next day. It was a Saturday, and it would be my last day with Jake. I was only here to give him advice on writing this school year and to collect my last paycheck from Kathy. Jake was hardly paying me any attention. His focus was going all into his sandwich and the television.

"Jake, at least pretend like you're listening, please."

Jake shut off the TV and turned toward me. "I'm sorry, babe, this show just calls to me." Jake took another huge bite of his food.

"Jake, have you learned anything from me being here?"

"Yeah, I've passed all my writing assignments, and I learned how depressing adulthood is." Jake spoke while chewing his food.

"Why do you say that?" I asked, puzzled.

"You talk about how miserable secrets are and how bad you feel for that Georgia lady and how much you like this Noah guy and how you have to hide all this stuff from him and yada yada."

I was shocked. "Jake! When did I tell you all that?"

"Everyday, Meaghan. You talk about it all the time. Can I turn my show back on?"

I nodded and said good-bye to Jake, who didn't even hear me leave. His mother was all in tears when I left, though, saying over and over how much she appreciated my help.

On my way to Georgia's I thought about Jake. I hadn't even remembered mentioning anything to him about my life, and yet he knew so much. I must have just been gabbing off, and then I recalled what Georgia had told me once, that you can never hide your thoughts. They'll eventually surface.

"Hey, you're here earlier than I had expected," Georgia was sitting on the porch, her white robe wrapped tightly around her. "It's lovely out today. I figured we'd just sit on the porch."

I pulled my notebook out and scribbled the date on the top right-hand corner. Georgia had been wearing the same outfit under the robe I had seen her in the previous day, which was very odd. She prided herself in how she looked. She would have something new on every day.

"Georgia, are you all right?"

She saw that I was looking at her jeans. "Oh, I'm fine. I was just too sore this morning to change my clothes. I feel great now. You ready to write?" she asked, changing the subject.

I shook my head yes.

"Okay, so I had been at Sophia's for about a year now. I was having so much fun, but the money I had saved in Vegas was slowly but surely winding down. I decided to go looking for a job, and Sophia had been kind enough to lend me her van. It was only a few miles into the city. I had restaurant and retail experience, so I applied to stores and a few restaurants. My last application was turned into this small thrift store. It was owned by a Mrs. Edith Elridge. She was around

sixty or so. She hired me on the spot, saying she needed any help she could get, and I looked honest enough. I started that day.

"She told me that she had a daughter who used to help her, but she ran off with a man to California, so she has had the store all to herself the past year.

"'I'm an old woman. I can't do everything as well as I used to. I could use your youth around here.'

"'I'm a hard worker. I'll do all that I can for you!'

I was so excited to have a job, I attached to Mrs. Elridge right away. She treated me like a daughter. She was so kindhearted and often gave away things in the store, saying they were off to a better home. I would go into work at eight in the morning and work until four when we would close. For a small thrift store, it would get quite busy during the week. We weren't opened on the weekends. Edith would attend church every Saturday and would visit the animal shelter every Sunday.

"I would often go to church and to the shelter with her on the weekends. She even began coming over for dinner with Sophia and I. Sophia, of course, always welcomed her with open arms, fainting at the sight of company."

The way I heard Georgia describe Sophia reminded me of my mother. I grabbed for my glass as Georgia continued.

"We all had a blast then. It's funny, though. I find that life is the scariest when everything is going so well, because you know a downfall is just around the corner."

I looked at Georgia, who was wiping her glasses with an orange handkerchief she had informed me Parker had given her as a token of his services in Vegas.

"What a pessimistic thought," I said.

Georgia laughed. "Is it? Well, I would say the best comparison of life is a rollercoaster, the ups and the downs and the flips. Think back on your own life. Could you disagree that when things couldn't get any better, they took a turn for the worst? Just think on it."

I pressed for her to continue.

"I had been working there for about six months. I went in one morning and found the ambulance and police hanging around. An officer about thirty years old or so with a thick brown mustache stopped me.

"'Can I help you?' he said with an authoritative voice.

"'I work here. Is everything all right?' I was searching the small crowd for Edith.

"'Well, ma'am, the old woman seemed to have had a heart attack this morning sometime. She didn't make it. I'd recommend you look for another job now. I just spoke to her daughter in California. She didn't have much to say, but she did mention she'd be selling this place right away.'

"I walked away from the store in disbelief. I had just been with Edith last night. She was all smiles at the dinner table. I drove straight home and fell weeping into Sophia's arms, who tried to calm me down for hours. I lay in bed that whole day, lying with Baby by my side, remembering Mrs. Elridge. I couldn't believe her daughter was just selling the place. I had heard Edith say several times how important the store was to er. It was practically a statue in the city. Sophia called me for dinner later in the evening.

"I was so angry at one point I told Sophia, 'Can she do that? I mean, can she just sell her mother's store?'

"'I'm afraid if it was willed to her then she could do whatever she pleases. Oh, Georgia, it was a great thing to know such a kind woman, but she's gone now, and you'll have to respect her family's decision to do what they want. I'm sure no matter how insincere her daughter sounded, it must be hard on her.'

"A very big light bulb had gone off in my head. 'A son, do you remember her speaking about a son that she had? What was his name?'

"'Noah?'

"'Yes! Noah! I mean he has to have some say in all this, doesn't he?'

"Sophia put her fork down. 'Well, I would suppose that he does, but he lives somewhere in Maine, she mentioned. I mean, she hadn't spoken to him in years, remember? And I don't even know what we would do, Georgia. We don't know where in Maine he lives, and we certainly don't have his phone number in our contact books.' Sophia laughed at the idea.

"'So we'll look him up! I mean, how many Noah Elridge's are living in Maine? I would imagine one!'

"Sophia smiled. 'Okay, so, you look him up, and let's say you find him, if he is even living in Maine anymore, because once again Edith hasn't talked to him in some time. But let's say you do find him. What are you going to say? Oh, I worked for your mother for a few months, and I was hoping you could convince your sister, whom

I've never met, to not sell the store. Could you do that for me stranger?' Sophia cupped her green mug and sipped the hot tea. 'Georgia, some things in life you just have to let go of. This isn't your family or my family. Let's respect our boundaries on this one, okay?'

"'Fine,' I said in defeat.

"The next day I had convinced Sophia to go over to Mrs. Elridge's house. I had been given a key so I could come over if I ever wanted to visit on the weekends, which I often had done. Sophia was against the whole idea.

"'So why are you standing in her house with me now?' I questioned.

"'Because I want to look for Noah's number too.'

"We both laughed. The house was dark now. The electricity had been shut off, and I could tell her family hadn't made their way to Jersey yet. Everything was in the exact spot as the last time I had visited. I had never been upstairs, and I had a feeling I would find what I was looking for up there. I remember Edith telling me about a book room on the second floor. She had said it was cluttered with boxes of old wish-wash, so I headed there first.

"Sophia and I had been smart enough to bring flashlights. I like felt I was in a Nancy Drew novel. Cluttered was an understatement to describe the state of the book room. There were boxes everywhere and two or three filing cabinets. While I was rummaging around, a small gold book caught my attention. In red cursive letters it read, 'Contacts.'

"'Sophia!' I yelled. 'I think I found it. Let's go!'

"I didn't open the book until we got home. Sophia made tea, and we sat at the bar in the kitchen. A thick rubber band bound it shut. I pulled it off, and it popped open like a children's pop-up book.

"'Look at these pictures. They're so old,' Sophia said, taking the four pictures that fell out of the front page. They were of Edith and her daughter and a young boy.

"When we saw him we both said, 'Noah!'

"It was not a difficult task finding his number. The contact book only had ten or so numbers, and there was only one Noah.

"'So you're going to call him, right?' I said to Sophia.

"'Me! This is your show, honey.'

"We both walked over to the phone, and I dialed the number. As soon as we heard the first ring I slammed the phone back onto the receiver.

"'What are you doing?' Sophia asked.

"'You were right. I don't know how to even start a conversation with him. What do I say?'

"'Just call. He might not even answer. It'll come to you if he does.'

"I looked at Sophia, so skeptical of what she had said.

"'Go on, dial,' she urged.

"The phone rang four times. I can still hear the rings. The silence in between each had my heart pounding, thinking I would hear his voice, but nothing happened.

"I turned to Sophia. 'He didn't answer.'

"We both sat down in disappointment.

"'Well, we did what we could, Georgia. The odds were against us finding him in the beginning.'

"Three days had passed after Edith Elridge's death. Sophia and I had attended the funeral. I had seen her daughter, who seemed to be a spitting image of Edith. She had the same grey eyes and the short blonde hair, which Edith's younger days had shown. Her skin was much darker than her mother's. The California sun had been kind to her. She wore a long green dress and was standing with a tall, handsome man wearing a black suit with a bright green tie. I had assumed that was the man Edith said she ran away with. I watched her all afternoon as she walked around the funeral parlor with a certain air about her. She was smiling and did not seem to have a care in the world for what had happened.

"After the service I followed her with Sophia by my side into the back part of the parlor to give her a piece of my mind. When we turned the corner, however, I saw her sit down beside her mother's closed casket and weep. She was holding her head in her hands and saying she was sorry over and over. Sophia and I looked at each other and turned back around.

"'I guess you never know what someone is really going through,' said Sophia.

"It was on our way outside that we came across a young, handsome man standing in front of a white car. His long black tie was loosened, and he stood with his hands in his pockets.

"'Sophia, I think, I think that's Noah.'

"'Sophia turned, squinting. 'By God, I think it is!'

"'Would it be indecent to say something to him?' I was speaking to Sophia while staring at the man. 'I think it would be rude of us to continue to stare and not say a word to him.'

"So Sophia and I walked over to the man who seemed to have his eyes focused on the stained-glass windows of the parlor.

"'Excuse me,' I said. The man turned his attention to me. 'Are you by any chance Noah Elridge?'

"'No, I'm Noah Harvest. I was given my father's name, not my mother's. I'm assuming you were close to Edith? Why, you must have been. I know no one but those few close to her would know of the existence of her son.' He laughed. His voice was like a long river in the desert valley—deep, raspy, and smooth.

"'Why is that?'

"'Well now, she left that part of the story out, didn't she?" He laughed again.

"Something about his laugh infuriated me. I felt a sudden burst of anger. I pushed his chest. 'Why are you laughing? Your mother is dead. Why are you acting like you don't care?'

"'Hey!' he yelled. 'I don't know what's going on here. Who the hell are you anyway?'

"I backed off and looked back at Sophia, who was shaking her head. 'I'm just some girl who worked for your mother and spent a good deal of time with her. I cared for her very much. It just angers me to see her two children walking around like they never had a mother.'

"'Jackie's in there?'

"'If Jackie is your sister, then yes. I never knew her name. Edith only mentioned yours.'

"He stared at me.

"'Well, I didn't mean to nudge into your business, but I had overheard a police officer saying that your sister was going to sell the store, and you see, I know how much the store meant to your mother. I was just hoping that you could make her reconsider. '

"Noah had laughed again but stopped once he saw my angry expression. 'The store is in my name. We all read the will this morning. I got the thrift store and the house. Jackie got some money. That's why I'm so shocked that she went in. She was pretty enraged when she left the lawyer's office. I live in Maine. I don't know what the hell I'm going to do with the house or the store, but I'll keep you updated since you were so dear to my mother, miss—'

"'Georgia, and this is Sophia. We live just up the street from Edith's.

"Sophia spoke up. 'Please feel free to come see us. We love company!'

"'Yeah, I'll see you around then,' he said, getting into his car.

"'Well, he seemed nice enough, and he was awfully handsome, don't you think?'

"I got into the van. 'He's far from charming,' I said.

"It was mid-week. I still wasn't used to not going to work. Sophia and I had been quieter than we normally were. I think we were so focused on Noah and what his moves were going to be that we hadn't made any moves for ourselves. It was cold outside. There had been light snowfall on the ground, and Sophia was having problems with the old heaters. Every hour or so, she would wander down to the basement to fix something. We had been walking around in chunky sweaters and long johns all day. We were sitting at the bar in the kitchen, sipping hot tea and watching the snow when we unexpectedly heard a loud knock on the door.

"'Who would be out here in this weather?' Sophia jumped and ran to the door.

"In moments Noah Harvest was sitting in the kitchen sipping hot tea with Sophia and me.

"'I thought I'd move down from Maine, figured it'd be warmer.' He laughed. 'But I guess I should've taken my chances in Maine. It's warmer outside in the snow then in here!'

"I laughed, and Sophia moaned. 'I know something's wrong with the heater in the basement. It's a million years old. I can't call anyone out here today. They won't come. We've got a snow storm on the way.'

"Noah stood. 'Well, where's your basement door? It wouldn't hurt if I had a look at it.'

"Sophia led him to the door, and in twenty minutes the house was toasty.

"Sophia praised Noah. 'It's so nice to have a handyman around here. This place is old. I try to keep up with everything, but it seems every season there's some mending somewhere I have to attend to.'

"'It's a marvelous home, though," Noah said, drinking coffee.

"'Did you say you moved down here?' I said.

"Noah and Sophia looked at me. I realized I had been quiet most of the conversation.

"'Yeah, I decided to go live at my mom's. I mean it's mine now.'

"'And the store?' I asked quickly.

"'The store, well, I haven't completely decided about that. I mean, I don't know anything about running a business. I'm just taking things slow for now. I know I have to do some maintenance work on the house. It's quite old as well, so that'll be my first task.'

"I went upstairs to my room. Sophia and Noah spent hours talking to each other. It wasn't until Baby ran out of my room that I saw Noah standing in the hall, looking for the bathroom.

"'She said upstairs to the right, right?'

"I laughed. 'Yes, it's that second one over there.'

"Baby was rubbing against his leg, purring. 'Cute cat, she yours?'

"'Yes, her name is Baby. She's real sweet. Do you have any pets?'

"'Yeah, a big German shepherd, actually. He was out in the car. Sophia let me bring him in. He's down in the kitchen if you'd like to see him.'

"I grabbed Baby. 'Yes, I believe I'll make my way down to see him.'

"As I started for the stairs, Noah turned, holding on to the banister. 'Why do you care for that store so much? I mean, it doesn't make a lot of profit. I've seen the papers, and it's not yours. I know you weren't rolling around in dough all day, so why care if I were to just sell the old place? I'd get more money selling it then keeping it.'

"I smiled. 'That's probably true, but when I worked with your mother, she said over and over how special that place was to her. She just had this passion about her. It was contagious. I would just hate to see all memory of her disappear.' I keep straight down the stairs and made my way toward the kitchen."

Chapter 14

I sat staring Georgia. "That's where we're stopping today? What about Noah? Can't we skip to the good stuff?"

Georgia laughed. "The good stuff?"

"Yes! You know the part where you and Noah fall in love and get married and have Noah Jr., the good details!"

"Ah, now if I told you everything in one day, why would you keep coming back? All in good time, Meaghan."

As if on cue, Noah pulled up. I put my notebook in my bag and stood.

Georgia looked up at me. "Are you leaving? It's only five. Why don't you stay a little longer?"

My eyes met with Noah's. He kissed my forehead and said, "Yeah, stay a little longer. I'll whip up something good to eat."

"I guess I can stay, it's early still." Georgia slowly stood and made her way into the house.

Noah pulled me back on the porch and kissed me harder. "You look beautiful today. How's everything? You seemed distant the other night."

I pushed him back a little. "I'm fine, just a few things on my mind, nothing to worry over."

"You want to talk about it? I'm here to listen, Meg."

"No," I said quickly. "I thought you were going to make a great dinner?" I smiled, changing the subject.

Noah opened the door, and I followed after. After a hearty meal, Noah walked me out to my car as custom.

"Could you stay with me tonight?" he asked. "I don't have to work tomorrow. We could just lay around all day."

I smiled. "Noah, what do you find attractive about me?" I laughed as he grabbed my bottom. "No, really, Noah. I mean, I'm terrible. I stopped talking to you for a while. I'm distant. I mean. What is attractive about that?"

Noah wrapped his strong arms around me. "I know that you're working on something in your head. I can see it in your eyes. I can see that it takes a toll on you. I understand if you don't want to talk about it, so I'm just going to hang around until you do want to. In the mean time, that gorgeous face and perfect body of yours keeps my interests up quite enough."

I laughed and kissed Noah the whole way to his bedroom. It rained all night, and all the next morning the heat from our bodies touching steamed up the windows. It was quite cold outside this morning. Noah stood reaching for his sweats. My eyes admired his toned body as he pulled up his pants. He looked over his shoulder, his eyes on my breasts.

He left, saying he'd be right back. In twenty minutes or so he creaked up the stairs with a platter of fruit, eggs, and toast for me. I hardly ate anything. I only hungered for his body. I hit euphoria making love to him all day and lying there, holding him afterward.

"Noah," I said softly, running my fingers through his hair. "I want to tell you everything, all the time. I just can't right now, you understand? I don't ever want to hide anything from you, it's just…"

He kissed my lips. "Meg, just tell me everything when you're ready. Just so you know, I'm here for you. I don't know how I can prove that enough. I love you, Meaghan." He kissed me once more.

My heart was fluttering. "I love you, Noah."

It was around eight when I finally left Noah's bed and climbed into the jeep. I came home and took a shower then lay on my futon with Lily, who I felt I hadn't seen in days. I closed my eyes, picturing Georgia sitting there with Noah and her cat Baby. I felt as if I were Georgia for a moment.

I wondered as I was editing everything I wrote this past week what had happened to Noah's father. I couldn't wait days to hear all the details. I figured I'd just ask Noah tomorrow and swear him to secrecy. I woke up around three in the morning. I heard someone in the kitchen. I thought it would be my father sneaking cookies again, so I decided to go join him. To my surprise I saw Bryan sitting at the table crying.

"Bry, what's wrong?" I asked, sliding around the corner.

He jumped. "Meg, I didn't know anyone was up. I'll just go upstairs."

I ran over to the table. "No, please sit. Come on, tell me what's up."

Bryan sat back down and wiped his eyes. "I went over to Cassie's today. Her mom told me she already left. I asked her where to, thinking she went out to the mall or something. Her mom just handed me this envelope and shut the door, so I sat in the car and read it.

Dear Bryan,

When you get this I will be landing in California. I decided to go to school out here in a bigger city. I told you Franklin was too small town for me, and honestly you are too. I think that you're a great guy, but I've been hanging out with someone who shares a bigger dream than cornfields and one-way roads, I'm moving in with him out here. Bryan, we had our fun. Please don't contact me after this. It'll only make things more difficult on yourself.

Cassie

I sat with my hands folded in my lap.

Bryan wiped more tears away and shook his head. "So of course I tried calling her a few times, and she just didn't answer, but Meaghan, I don't understand. I mean, we were hanging out and great yesterday! Yesterday, Meaghan! How the hell does all this happen in one day?"

I looked down. "A lot can happen in a day, Bry."

"Really, Meaghan? I'm just in awe. I want to go out there after her so bad."

"Bryan, don't do that. It's not there. If she was dumb enough to just leave a great guy like you, I mean, she's been feeling that way for some time now."

Bryan cut me off. "What do you mean some time? How would you know?"

I realized the anger in his eyes. I had let something slip, and it was too late for recovery. "That day I went to the mall with her, Bryan, she said some things…"

"What things?" Bryan was yelling at this point. My parents had turned on the lights and were walking down the stairs in their robes, asking what was going on.

Bryan's eyes never left mine. "What things, Meaghan? What was she saying? You mean you knew this was all going to happen and you didn't care to inform your brother?"

"Bryan, I—"

"No, Meaghan."

My mother covered her mouth. "Bryan, watch your mouth."

"I loved her, and you didn't care to mention something to your own brother? Nothing? You just sit there so innocent like there isn't a world around you. What if it was Noah? What if Noah just left and I knew about it?"

"Bryan, I didn't know she was going to leave today and go to California, Jesus!"

"No, but you knew she'd be leaving. What if Noah left, Meg? Answer the question!" Bryan pounded on the table.

"I wouldn't be sitting here crying all night," I said coldly.

Bryan stormed up the stairs.

My mother was calling up the stairs for him. All I heard was the door slam. My father stood there demanding to know what was going on.

"Cassie left him, Dad. She's in Cali now with some guy, and I knew about it. I'm a terrible person. Go on, scorn me. Both of you tell me how much of a screw up I am." I stood and walked back down to my futon.

I sat there until six or seven in the morning with my eyes swollen and my head hanging low. Then I fell asleep. I dreamt of Noah and I making love. I heard him whisper I love you over and over again. I saw goose bumps crawling up my legs as I held his back, my hands digging in to his skin while I uncontrollably let out moans. It was the most peaceful, most sensual dream I could ever remember having, and then in the corner of the room, I saw Georgia standing. She looked so sickly, and she held hair in her hands.

That's when I woke up and saw Lily and my alarm clock flashing 11:05. I hadn't the energy to pull out the futon last night, so I lay with my legs hanging over the end and my blanket wrapped tightly around me. I was hungry after a while of sitting there, but I didn't want to walk upstairs. I didn't want to see my parents, and especially Bryan. I took a quick shower, wrapped my hair into a high bun, and sat in front of my mirror, trying my hardest to conceal the redness under my tired eyes. I had texted Noah asking him to meet me at the café for some breakfast. He was the only person I could stand seeing right now.

It was cold out this morning. I wore black leggings, a black tank top, my green army jacket, and my white converse. I threw my messenger bag around my shoulder and waved back to Noah, who was sitting inside by the window waving at me. His smile was big. I could tell he was happy by my rare text to hangout somewhere.

"Hey," he said, standing and kissing me as we sat.

I had ordered coffee and croissants.

"I was surprised you wanted to see me this morning. I know you like keeping to yourself."

"Of course I wanted to see you. You're my boyfriend, aren't you?" My tone was so bland and low, but I saw the excitement in Noah's eyes.

"Yes, yes, I am. Well, what's on your mind? You look kind of tired."

I smiled. "Kind of tired, well I guess this concealer is doing its job, because I'm beyond tired." I laughed, and Noah grabbed my hand.

"Talk to me. What's up?"

I smiled. It's a touching thing to hear someone ask you to tell them all your worries. "I'm just the biggest idiot. I'm a terrible, terrible person, Noah. My brother's girlfriend, who he really, genuinely loved, she just up and left him, and get this, I knew that she didn't want to be with him forever like he wanted to be with her. She told me that, and I didn't say anything, not one word to him about it. He's my brother, Noah. He's my brother, and I didn't tell him." I took a deep breath. "What is wrong with me?"

I saw Noah's eyes searching for the right thing to say. "Well, that's a hard thing. I mean to tell someone something that harsh. You obviously care for your brother in the sense that you knew it would hurt him, and that's why you didn't tell him, but—"

I cut him off, pulling my hand away from his. "But he's my brother, and I still should have told him, yeah, I get it."

Noah sat back in the booth.

I could tell he wanted to change the subject, so I did. "Where's your dad, if you don't mind me asking?" I said, sipping my coffee.

"My dad, I'm not real sure. I mean, my mom doesn't say much about him. I remember being around him when I was little, and then there was just one day when he wasn't there, and my mother didn't speak on it." Noah put his elbows on the table and cupped his hands together.

"You never cared to question her about it?" After the question slid off my tongue, I could tell my tone was too aggressive.

Noah laughed. "Well, yeah, I mean once or twice when I was younger, but she never gave me a straight answer." Noah smirked. "It's kind of like if you brought something up to someone and you knew it would hurt them."

I picked up my coffee. "Yeah, yeah, I get it."

Noah's bright smile was contagious, like his mother's. I found myself laughing a little the harder I tried to hide my smile.

"What made you ask about my father?"

"Well," I said, scheming in my mind. "I figured you met my father. I was just wondering why I hadn't met yours, but I understand he's not in your life. I was just curious." I looked up to see if he bought it. I only wanted to know because I wanted a head start on the story, and I realized again in that moment how diabolic I was. I was trying to get information from the man I loved to have a foot up on his dying mother. "Lord," I whispered.

"What?" Noah said. "Well, I have to get back to work. Are you going to my mom's?"

"Yeah," I said, standing with my coffee in my right hand. He kissed me, and I slowly let go of his hand as he got into his truck.

"I'll see you later all right?"

"All right!" I said.

I sat in my car for about fifteen minutes before I drove to Georgia's. I went over with the intent to speed through her story until she got to her and Noah, but I'd learned Georgia to be a stand firm kind of woman. Any attempt at me passing the details failed.

"Sophia and I, after winter had passed and spring was settling in, were helping Noah around his new home almost every day. If he wasn't with us at Sophia's, then we were with him. Toward the end of spring when everything with the house seemed finished, Noah brought up the store to me outside one afternoon.

"'I want to keep the store opened, make a few changes to it, and see how it goes for one year. If it does well, I'll keep it. If it goes the other way, well, then I'll sell it.'

"I clapped in excitement.

"'I also thought I'd be an idiot if I didn't ask you to come back and work.' He looked at me, smiling.

"I quickly agreed, and by the end of June that year, the store had been re-opened with lots of new furnishings and a modern set up. Noah was a great businessman. He learned the ropes of the store quickly and found new ways to bring in customers all the time. I admired his work ethic."

I smiled. "That's not all you admired, is it?"

Georgia laughed. "We had been working very hard that summer, and the holidays kept us busy. It wasn't until next winter when we slowed down. The snow kept almost everyone home, but Noah and I were still coming in. It was in those slow and almost silent months that we grew close. He was picking me up from Sophia's and driving me into the store. We spent all day together. He told me about his childhood, how him and his sister never got along and how his mother was hard on him.

"'She portrayed me as my father. I guess we looked a lot alike, and she would often say that she hated seeing me because she saw him. Hearing that as a kid is tough, you know? Your mother tells you that she hates seeing you, and your sister is held up on a pedestal.' He laughed. 'In fact, I moved when I was eighteen and got a few roommates in Maine until I could afford my own apartment. She didn't call me for years, and I stopped caring. It wasn't until my sister messed up in my mother's eyes and ran off with some guy to Cali. I'm sure she told you about that.'

"I shook my head yes, indulged in the story.

"'Yeah, we spoke consistently for a while and then stopped. She said she just couldn't listen to my voice without seeing my father. The next phone call I got was from her lawyer telling me I needed to come down to Jersey and have a look at her will. No one called me to tell me my mom had passed. As you imagine, I put the puzzle together myself.' Noah sat down on one of the display chairs.

"'Did you ever ask why the memory of your father hurt her so much?'

"He smirked. 'He left her for her best friend, apparently. What kind of monster would do that?'

"My heart sank. I immediately told him of my mother's story and my story, all about Elaine and my father and the people I'd encountered on the way. He admired my story and how much we had in common, even the little things like our favorite color, yellow, and we both preferred desert before the main course."

Georgia laughed and waved her hand as if she were shooing away the memory. "We really hit it off back then."

"So what happened?" I asked, my eyes big.

"A few nights the rides on the way home were terrible. We had to drive so slow because of the snow. A few nights it had snowed so bad that I couldn't believe we made it to the house. I would stay with Noah. The first night I insisted I lay on the couch. The second night I slept in the upstairs guest room, and the third night and all those to follow I found myself only comfortable in his arms."

"And then…" I said, smiling.

"And then—" Georgia laughed. "And then he told me he loved me after a few months. It was warm outside now. There was no snow. Bad weather could no longer be my excuse for spending the night. I had told Sophia that we were a thing, you know? It wasn't much longer after that when Noah had asked me just to move everything into his place, and it wasn't much longer after that when I was nine months pregnant with a baby boy."

"So you were in love?"

Georgia smiled. I realized I sounded like a little girl wanting to hear the rest of the princess story. "Yes, I was very much in love, and nothing could have been more perfect. We had a large home, the store was doing well enough for Noah to keep it open, and my best friend Sophia was always there. It was like one big fairy tale."

Georgia pointed to the window. The cold wind outside had blown it open a little. She pulled her sweater close to her, and I closed the window.

"What happened after you had Noah?"

Georgia grabbed her coffee mug and blew the top. Steam rose and disappeared into the ceiling. "Well, remember when I told you that life is scary when it's going good?"

I shook my head yes.

"I had Noah in October that year. He was healthy and handsome. I held him so tight every day. I swore I would never let anything happen to him. Noah Sr. at the time seemed quite distant. I had heard of mothers having depression problems after birth, but not fathers. I had asked him one evening after putting Noah to sleep what was the matter.

"He looked up at me, tired and worn. 'I'm just a bit overwhelmed, I suppose.' He said nothing more on the matter.

"It was weeks before I was in the shop again. Noah had told me not to worry about anything, that Sophia would be cashiering, and I didn't worry about anything. I was at home with the best thing life had given me. When I did go back to the store, business was slow. It was nearing winter, and we would go days without one customer. It was slow the previous year, but this was just miserable! Noah started telling me not to even bother coming to the store.

"One night in particular, he came in around eleven or so, which was extremely late, because we closed at six. As soon as I met him at the door, I smelt the strong aroma of whiskey. I could remember my Uncle John smelling of it often.

"'Where have you been, Noah? I've been worried all night!'

"He waved me away, but I persisted.

"'That worthless store. I knew I should have just sold it. It never made much profit from the beginning, that's why all my mother had was this shack.'

"'This shack, Noah? This is our home, and it's wonderful. Since when is it a shack?'

"He put his hand around the back of his neck. 'Georgia, I have been paying the bills for the store out of my own pockets. The store hasn't made one dollar for three months now. I can't afford to pay for the store and pay for the house and pay for our son and pay for the car and pay for food!' He stood, yelling with his finger in the air.

"'Noah,' I whispered, wrapping my hands around his waist. 'Please sit down. We'll figure it out. I promise.'

"He kissed my forehead and walked upstairs to our bedroom. When I went up minutes later, he was fast asleep. I took his boots off and his coat and held him until morning, running my fingers through his hair."

Chapter 15

I walked toward the fridge, searching for the scallions to hand off to Georgia, who was making mashed potatoes and had a pot roast slow cooking all afternoon. The hearty aroma filled the entire house. I watched Georgia hold on to the table, the chairs, and the counter like a wobbly toddler learning how to walk. She kept insisting on me sitting rather than giving her the help she most definitely needed.

When Noah had arrived, everything was done. I found myself hardly talking and listening in and out of conversations. I stayed late enough to help clean up, and then I was being escorted to my car by Noah as usual. Bryan was standing on the porch when I got home. He turned right around, and I watched him walk upstairs as I came in.

My mother stood at the entryway to the kitchen. "Meaghan, could you come here?"

I walked into the kitchen to see my mother toss the old coffee grounds from the day. "You know I hate when you and your brother fight. Now please could you go reconcile with him?" My mother flattened down the front of the pink ruffled apron I had always seen her in.

"Mom, he doesn't want to talk to me. Maybe in a few days I'll try. As of right now it's a no go."

It was October now. I had wanted to get Noah something special for his birthday, so I wandered down to the harvest fest in the town center. There were always lots of people there for the festival. My mother's store was full and so were the concession stands. I walked down to the one store I hadn't really seen a crowd in front of; it was Elias's Books. I had recalled going there once before back when I was in high school. There were hundreds, maybe even more books stacked neatly in shelves, and then there were books just stacked everywhere. I got the idea to pick up a few old ones for Noah to read. I was looking for the old Peter Pan I remember he told me his mother read to him when he was little.

When I had found everything I was looking for, I headed to my mother's store to see if I could help any. I ended up cashiering most of the evening. I heard some women in line talking to my mother about Georgia. They were saying how sickly she looked now and how they knew something was different about her.

"And her hair!" another woman said, referring to how little she had now.

My mother tried to change subject by offering 10 percent off, which was approved with the ahhs from all the ladies. I stood at the register feeling like I was having déjà vu of Georgia's story. I felt as if I were her, and my mother was her Aunt Loretta. It wasn't the first time I had felt this way.

Later that night I gave Noah his books and a small cake I had picked up for him. I spent the night, and we had sex several times.

"This is one birthday for the books," he said after we had finished.

I laughed and lay beside him with my hand on his sweaty chest. "I do love you, Noah," I said, laying my head on his chest and looking into his eyes.

"I love you to, Meg. You all right?"

"Yeah, I feel great laying here with you." I kissed his soft lips.

We just lay there for a while talking about anything, and then Noah said after our laughter had ceased, "Do you notice anything different about my mom?"

I looked at him and then looked away, putting my head under his arm. "What are you talking about?"

"Nothing, I don't know. I had a few guys at work ask about my mom. I guess their wives were saying she looked sick. I haven't noticed anything really, but I mean, I see her every day, you know? Then I came home after work today and saw her standing in the kitchen. I watched her grab on to the counter like it was the only thing keeping her standing. I noticed she lost weight too. I saw her beside an old picture hanging on the fridge. I asked her if she was okay, and of course she said yes. I don't know, Meg. What do you think? I mean maybe I'm just noticing something that's not even there just because someone's wife thinks she looks sick."

I heard my heart pounding as I lay there in silence. It occurred to me after a long pause that I needed to say something, and like a seducing snake, I whispered into his ear, "I think you need to get on top of me again."

Noah kissed me, smiling.

He lay sound asleep, and I lay there rubbing his chest. I felt a tear run down my cheek. I wondered how much longer he'd want to see me after Georgia told him.

Christmas rolled around. I had made time to spend half the day with my family and the other half with Noah and Georgia. Noah had gone over to my parents for a little while, and Georgia and I stood in her kitchen mashing potatoes and slicing cranberry sauce.

"I remember my first Christmas with Noah. He was just a baby, but we had a small tree, maybe four feet or so. It was just as grand as the big ones. He stared at the lights in amazement. It was such a fun time, a temporary detour from everything we had to deal with any other day. Sophia had gotten me some beautiful sweaters, and Noah got me a gold chain bracelet. I wondered how he afforded it, but I never asked. His smile was so proud. I didn't want to hurt him." Georgia smiled, looking down at a thin gold bracelet.

I touched it. "It's beautiful. He did a good job."

"It was a good day. Christmas has always been a lovely time for me. I remember Loretta had phoned me wishing us all a merry Christmas. She couldn't believe I was a mother now. She was crying on the phone when she heard Noah's coos and told me my mother would be so proud to call me her daughter, and now he's all grown up, and he has a great woman to share all this with. Nothing could make me happier."

I smiled and lay plates out on the table. It was a picturesque evening. It had snowed all day, and all I saw were the decoration lights shining through the windows. I had gotten Georgia a silver necklace with a diamond at the end, a rarity in my mother's store. I had gotten Noah boots for work and a wool cardigan. Noah gave me diamond earrings, and Georgia gave me the softest quilt I have ever had. Georgia had kept the festivities going until midnight or so, and when she finally went off to bed, I saw her looking back at the tree. It hadn't occurred to me until that moment that this would be her last Christmas.

I cuddled up to Noah that night, my fingers running through his hair. I closed my eyes to see Georgia running her fingers through Noah Sr.'s hair, thinking over all the problems in head, trying to find a solution to tomorrow.

The next morning Noah was off to work with my father, and I made my way downstairs to the kitchen. I put on a pot of coffee and sat at the table with Georgia. She had a sweater on and two quilts lying on her lap. The heat in the house had me sweating, and she was shivering. I grabbed my tablet, and we picked up where we left off.

"Noah sold the store and Edith's home, and we moved to Maine where he had been living into the very apartment complex he had left. I remember unpacking everything. It was smaller than the house, of course, but it was a fine home, and it was ours. I had hardly seen Noah in those days. He was going back and forth from New Jersey to Maine. He said he had papers for the store and the house to sign and send to all types of people, so I had spent most of my time decorating the apartment, wallpapering it, and painting the window sills.

"I cared for our son every day. Noah hardly saw him, and it was later after Noah's second birthday that I

questioned why he was still going to Jersey every week.
The house had been sold for over a year now, the same
with the store, and it was then he fell to the floor in
tears saying that he wasn't in love with me, saying that
he was in love with Sophia and that he had been staying with her there and coming back to me in Maine
just long enough to give me money he had made from
lumbering and the little he made from the house and
the store.

"It was then that I took Noah and the car and
just drove off in tears, filled to the brim with anger.
I remembered Candice. I drove until I ran out of gas,
which took me to the small town of Franklin, Maine."

Georgia had never spoken so fast. I could tell it was
still painful to her.

"So you just stayed here? What made you stay?
Where did you go?"

Georgia asked me for more coffee, and she spoke as
I poured.

"Well I was sitting around the corner from a gas
station. I just made it to fill up with the little money I
had. It's a small town around here, as you know. There
was a woman who used to own Herb's gas station with
her husband, Herb. She knew I was new around here,
and she fell for Noah. She asked me where I was staying, and I said I didn't know. Unexpectedly, this woman,
whose name was Lillian, begged Noah and I to stay
with her, and we did. She was the sweetest woman I
had ever met."

"What did you and Noah do?"

"I started cashiering in the front of the gas station. Lillian held Noah all day long, and he learned how to pump when he was around five or six." Georgia laughed. "He thought he was the coolest kid on the block."

Georgia looked down at her silver watch. I hadn't seen her wear it in sometime. She told me she needed to go somewhere. I offered to drive her, but of course she refused, so after she left, I followed her for a little ways. The trees that passed were familiar, and when she turned around the bend, I saw she was heading to the river my father had taken me to. I continued to drive straight rather then follow her. I headed home, wondering what she was doing down there.

Since the confrontation with my brother, I had been going back to my roots of sneaking in the back door and only going upstairs after I heard him leave. My mother had addressed the issue several times, asking us to shake hands and get over it, but each time my brother and I would just turn and go our separate ways.

Today was no different. It had been months since our quarrel. At first I felt guilty and terrible. At this point I was just as infuriated. We both saw each other getting out of our cars. He took the front door. I went around back. Not one word was uttered. No eye contact was made.

I sat in my room until dinner. I was editing the writing I had done today, flipping through all the pages I had collected. I sighed, realizing we were getting to the end.

Noah came over at night. I had given him my spare key to come in any time he wanted to. I was already asleep when he arrived. I woke up the next morning feeling his warm body wrapped around mine.

"Good morning, lovely," he whispered.

"Good morning," I said, kissing his lips. "You want to get dressed and go out for some breakfast?"

I yawned and worked my way to the bathroom to get ready. When I came back in, Noah was fast asleep again. I kissed his forehead and decided I'd go to the café solo to get some coffee and bring it back. I ran into Kathy, Jake's mom, inside. She ordered a chi tea and went on to tell me how much Jake's writing had improved this school year.

"Jake's a great kid. It was all him. He put in so much hard work." I gave Jake all the credit as I hoped he would give me credit someday. It was nice to hear from someone how much my work was appreciated.

I thought on my way back home to Noah about what I would do with Georgia's story. It was only meant to be a treasure for Noah, but I wanted it to be something so much bigger. Then the thought came to me to have it published. I decided I'd discuss it with Georgia this afternoon.

"Hey, I must have fallen asleep. Thanks for the coffee." Noah was sitting up. His hair looked like the aftermath of a whirlwind.

"No worries, you looked so tired I just had to let you sleep in. When did you come in last night?" I said, sipping my hot tea.

"Around eleven or so. I couldn't sleep in my bed without you, so I came over. I watched a Twilight Zone marathon until I fell asleep."

I laughed. "Yeah, it was still playing this morning. I woke to, 'You're now going into the Twilight Zone.' I thought, Geez."

We both laughed. Then Noah stood. He had spilt a little coffee down his chest. I grabbed a towel from the bathroom and was interrupted by my mother's knocking.

"Meaghan, you got mail! It's from New York!"

"Oh joy," I mumbled. "My landlord is probably taking me to court." I grabbed the letter and threw it on the pool table.

Noah was off to work, and I was off to Georgia's.

"You want to get my story published?" Georgia said with a skeptical glance as she poured tea into the dingy floral cups.

"Yes, I mean with your permission, of course. I was just leafing through everything last night, and I thought about how incredible your story is. I just feel it could be something bigger."

"It's not supposed to be something big. I just wanted something I could give to Noah. He used to ask about my past all the time, and I never had the courage to tell him anything. I appreciate what you're trying to do, honey, but I just want it to be something for Noah to keep close to his heart."

I sunk in my chair. My determination wouldn't let me drop the matter. "Georgia, you are an incredible woman. Please let me do this for you and for Noah. Please?" I tried to put on the biggest puppy dog eyes I could muster up.

Georgia smiled while running her hands over the placemat on the table. "I trust you, Meaghan. I want you to promise me that this story will be told the same as I told it, and Noah has to read it first. When the time is right, then you may publish it one hundred times over."

I hugged Georgia tightly. "Thank you!"

Chapter 16

I came home one February night. At the same time I was pulling into the driveway, my mother came running outside.

"Meaghan! Meaghan! Noah just called. He wanted to know if you were here yet." My mother was in a frenzy.

"What's wrong?" I asked, putting the jeep in park.

"Noah's at the hospital with Georgia. He said she's collapsed. He sounded so worried."

"What? I just came from there. She was fine." My voice faded as those last words slipped out of my mouth. I knew Georgia wasn't fine. She hadn't been fine for months.

"All right, Mom. I'm going to go over there."

I flipped the car in reverse and speedily made my way toward the hospital. I found myself shaking as I parked. Warm tears fell down my cheeks. I didn't know if I could look at Noah. It would only be a matter of time until the doctors told him she had cancer.

I walked into the main lobby and asked for her room. I then found my way down the hall, scanning each door number until I came to 1F. I saw Noah sitting beside her bed with his head down. I tapped on the door lightly.

Noah stood and opened it. "Thank you for coming," he said, wrapping his arms around me.

"I came as soon as my mom told me. Is she all right?" I asked.

"Well, all I know is that she collapsed from exhaustion, or that's what she told me. She already spoke with a few doctors, but she won't let them tell me anything until you get here. I don't understand why she wants to wait for you, but by all means, I'm happy you're here."

I didn't want to go in the room. I knew why she was waiting for me, but I went in anyway with a tear or two streaming down my face. She asked Noah to stand outside and shut the door. She looked sicklier than when I had seen her earlier today. The blankets on the bed swallowed her small body. The white paint against the gray bedframe made her skin look gray and worn. The only thing that assured me it was Georgia I was looking at was the big grin she gave me when I made my way to the right side of her bed.

"Georgia?" I said like a frightened child peering around the corner.

"Sit down, honey. Now listen. I need you to listen to every word I tell you. I'll be going home tomorrow. They have to keep me overnight for observation," she complained, lifting up her IV. "The doctors insisted on telling Noah, you know."

I stopped her. "You know what, Georgia? I don't know what the hell I'm doing here. I don't know why you insisted on telling everyone you were waiting on me to get here. So you could get me to tell Noah, or so I could back you up for waiting so long to tell him?"

I cupped my hands over my mouth. My tears were continuous now. "I can't do this anymore, Georgia. I love Noah. I love him so much, and every time he asks if you look different or if there's anything wrong with you, I lie. I'm not lying to him anymore. You have cancer, and you are dying. You can't even say those words. You are so stubborn. I'm going to finish your story for Noah, and then I'm out whether you're still here or not. Now I'm going to open that door, and I'm going to let your son in here, and you have to tell him. You have to tell him now, or I'm telling him. Either way, it's happening tonight."

Without hesitation, and despite the astonished look on Georgia's face, I opened the door with tears strolling down my face and let Noah in.

"What's going on?" he asked, looking at me.

I just pointed to the chair, and he sat down, looking from me and back to his mother.

"Ma are you all right?"

I stood at the end of her bed.

She looked at me and then to Noah. Georgia grabbed his hand. "Noah, I want you to listen to me and then ask questions, okay? But please just listen to me."

He looked up to me as I wiped my tears. "I have cancer, Noah. I've had it for a while, and now, well, it's catching up to me is all. I didn't want to worry you. That's why I haven't told you until now, and I wasn't going to tell you tonight until, well, Meaghan insisted that I did. I've been working with Meaghan on a book, a story of my whole life for you. For months we've been working on it, and Meaghan's going to have it published, isn't that wonderful?" Georgia said smiling.

I could tell Noah was angry. "You waited to tell me you have cancer? Jesus ma, so what now? I mean do, you do chemo? What? What do we do?" Noah was standing with his hands in the air.

I continued to cry as Georgia waved her arms, asking him to sit.

"Noah, please be quiet. I'm not doing any of that. It's too late now."

"So what, ma? You expect me to just sit around while you die? Is that your plan, ma?" He turned to me. "And you, how could you not tell me? You knew this all along? You knew she was going to die, and you didn't say anything?"

I covered my mouth, sobbing.

"Noah, please honey, it's not her fault. I begged her not to tell you."

Noah continued to yell until two doctors and a security guard came into the room. They asked me to leave, so I waited for an hour until Noah came storming out through the waiting room into the parking lot. I followed, calling his name. When he reached his truck, he stopped, but only to pull the keys from his pocket.

"Noah, please, will you listen to me for a minute?"

"Listen to you, about what? More lies, Meaghan, because that's all you've been telling me so far. You know I tried. I actually cared to impress you, and God, if you only knew how much I gave to be with you, everything I did for you. Every time we went out to eat I got to reserve those for us because I did extra work for the guy for free. I told you I loved you. I invited you into my home with my mother, and you knew everyday that she was getting worse all those times I asked you. All you did was lie to me. Just leave, Meaghan.

"I saw that letter from New York a ways back. I was too curious to let it sit there, so I read it and put it back in the envelope. You got a job offer for a paper back in New York. You have enough money now from my mom, don't you? Just go on. Leave. Run back to New York and forget about this little town like you did before. Go find your next victim to write about. Maybe it'll be a bestseller."

Noah was speeding off into the night before I could protest to anything. I walked back to my car. I pulled up to my house, and in a fit of anger hit my steering wheel and then pulled my messenger bag around my shoulder.

My mother was waiting up to hear what had happened. I hadn't the energy to explain it all, so I told her Georgia was fine, and I'd tell her all about it tomorrow. I found my brother waiting for me in the basement. When I made my way down the steps, he flipped off the TV and sat up.

"What the hell are you doing in my room?" I asked, throwing my bag on the pool table.

Bryan laughed. "Jesus, I just wanted to talk for a minute."

"What, you want to go over how bad of a person I am? Because that won't be necessary. I already had that fact reiterated tonight." I sat on my vanity chair facing Bryan. I began to cry again.

"What's wrong? I haven't said anything yet."

I was sobbing. "Noah hates me, his mother hates me, you hate me. I just can't do anything right for myself."

Bryan wrapped his arm around me. It had been a long time since he'd done that. "I don't hate you, Meg.

I was just angry at myself. I should have seen Cassie leaving. She talked about it so much. It was just easier for me to put the blame on someone else, so that's what I did." Bryan stood tall as I wiped away my tears.

"I'm still not over her. I know it's going to take some time, but I was thinking today that in the meantime I might as well restore our relationship."

I hugged him. "Thank you, Bryan. I really needed this. I swear to you I didn't know she was going to run off to Cali with some guy."

"Yeah, I know. I was just pissed, Meg. So what's all this about Noah and his mom?"

Bryan sat back on the futon, and for the next hour and a half I rattled off my whole story. He sat in silence when I was done.

"See, it's that bad. You haven't said a word yet." I shook my head.

"Well, Meg, I'm not pointing fingers, but you promised Georgia you'd keep her business between you and her. Then you started seeing Noah. I'd say he's like me. He's pissed his mother wasn't telling him the truth, and he's pissed that she's dying, and he can do nothing about it. He's just looking for someone to blame right now, and by God, it's you."

Bryan went off to bed a little while later. I sat in my sweats, watching TV until finally I was able to doze off, which was a little around four.

I called Noah over and over and over. He never answered. I left a dozen voicemails he never returned. I wanted to drive over to his home so badly, but I figured he wouldn't come out. Laying on my futon surrounded by used Kleenexes, I wondered how this was all going to play out. I knew from the beginning this was going to be a sour ending, it just snuck up on me faster than I had anticipated.

Any vibration that came from my phone had me dashing across the room to pick it up, only be disappointed by an incoming email or a warning to plug in my dying phone. I didn't come up for lunch or dinner. I found myself sitting in the kitchen at three or four in the morning heating up leftovers. I didn't want to talk to anyone about anything except for Noah. All I wanted to do was explain myself.

When I returned to the basement, the torn envelope Noah had spoken about from New York caught my eye. Its edge was poking out from behind some old books my father had in the bookcase about how to run a pool hall. I figured Noah must have hid it there, thinking I would actually want to leave him and go to New York. I shook my head at the thought. After reading the letter, I slid it back into the envelope and fell asleep wearing Noah's baseball tee.

—⁂—

Valentine's Day passed. I had gotten Noah a small gift the day of Georgia's hospital visit. I sat fumbling it around in my hands with my phone to my ear, listening to Noah's phone ring and ring and ring. I had cried all the tears I had to cry the past few days. My face was dry, my eyes were sore and red, and my heart ached. This was worse than being alone on Valentine's Day.

My brother and my father had gotten me roses. I sat them in a tall crystal vase my mother had under the sink. I put them on my nightstand. The light from my lamp gave a shine to the ruby petals. There was nothing on TV except for marathons of the greatest romance movies. They played love songs on the music channels, and I didn't dare go for a walk in fear of seeing hearts and cupid posted up all around town.

The days following were just as lonesome. I finally got up the courage to drive on over to Georgia's to see Noah. When I pulled up he was just getting out of his truck. He turned to see me pull in, and for a moment I could have sworn he smiled. When I got closer I could see his face was dark and angry.

Chapter 17

"Hey," I began.

Without hesitation he continued walking through the garden as if he hadn't heard my voice.

"Noah? You can't keep walking away from me. You're being childish."

He turned and laughed. "I'm being childish?"

I hadn't heard his voice in some time. It sent chills up my back.

"I'd suggest you go home, Meaghan. I have nothing to say to you." He turned, buttoning his jacket. There was still a cold winter breeze lingering.

"Well, I have something to say to you, Noah Harvest. The only reason I didn't tell you a thing was because I promised your mother first that I wouldn't breathe a word, and it wasn't my place to say anything to you anyway."

Noah turned, staring at me. "You really think you didn't do anything wrong, don't you? Jesus, I can hear it in your voice." He shook his head while I put my hands in my sweater pockets. "Meg, I cared for you, and you were lying this whole time. How do I know if anything you said was ever truthful? As far as I'm concerned, it was all lies."

I was furious and felt tears building up behind my stone face. "Noah, how can you say that? I was honest about everything I said to you about us. I just didn't want to hurt you."

He laughed hysterically, cutting me off. "You didn't want to hurt me? How do you think I feel now? My mother is laying in there, and I'm just hanging around until she's dead, because it's too late to do anything now, and maybe if someone would have mentioned all this to me months ago, there'd be a hell of a better chance I could have convinced her to get treatment." He waved his hands, and I saw a tear slide down his worn face.

"Noah, you really think I have anything to do with your mother's illness, like you or I could have prevented all this? Listen to me, please. I miss you. I haven't sleep hardly at all. All I think about is you, and I understand that I didn't go about all this the best way, but you have to believe what I'm saying to you. I love you, Noah." I saw my breath as I spoke in the cold air.

"Meaghan, you need to go home now. There's nothing more to discuss."

I walked to my jeep and grabbed the pages of Georgia's story I had written. They were bound together by string, and I walked right up to Noah and threw the packet at his feet. "Here, this is from your mother. She's an incredible woman, and hopefully after you read all that's there you'll see it too. I'm taking that job in New York. I'm going to leave and forget about this little town and all the people in it like before. I'm taking your advice, Noah." I stormed off into the car, slamming the door and hitting my gas petal.

For weeks I sat in my room watching television, not eating much and sleeping a lot. I read and reread my invitation from New York. When I had told Noah that I would leave I didn't mean it. I hadn't even thought about it until recently. I hadn't heard from Noah since we argued, and I hadn't heard from Georgia.

One night I was going through some old clothes when my phone started to vibrate on top of the pool table. It was Georgia Harvest. I answered my phone immediately.

"Hello?"

"Meet me by the old lake. The story isn't finished." There was a click at the other end.

I wasted no time to grab a light jacket, grab my bag and my keys, and make my way down to the lake I had been to dozens of times with my father but never Georgia.

The twenty-minute drive felt like an eternity. I didn't play music on the way. I didn't stop off anywhere. I was so focused on getting there I wanted to hear what Georgia had to say. When I pulled up I wasn't sure what pavilion I needed to go to until I saw Noah's truck. I had figured Georgia took it alone, and then I saw Noah's outline down by the pavilion, that read, "B3."

I pulled my messenger bag over my shoulder and slowly walked down the hill to the lake. I was thankful I wore my sneakers. Anything else would have had me sliding down the hill. The setting seemed to be something out of a horror film.

Georgia stood fragile and white in a pink robe that swallowed her body. Her hair was in tight curlers, and her glasses reflected the light from Noah's flashlight. Georgia was holding on to the edge of the wooden table. She waved us to sit.

"I'm glad you came, Meaghan. I thought it inappropriate to speak on anything without the representation of my writer." She smiled, which made me chuckle a little, and then Noah's angry eyes met mine.

Georgia tugged Noah's jacket to sit down.

"I read the story, Meaghan." Georgia spoke with her tiny hands crossed. "It was lovely. I felt I was back at every place in my past. All the emotions came swarming back to me, but when I got to the end, I realized I hadn't told you the rest of the story. I mean, I had realized it before. I just decided not to tell you." Georgia looked down, and I saw Noah look up at me. His eyes were much softer now.

I pulled out my yellow tablet and my black ink pen I had been so accustomed to using. I hadn't written anything for weeks, so the pen felt almost foreign in between my fingers. I swirled a few small circles across the margin of the paper until I got the feel for writing back. It also felt strange having Noah sitting across from me. Out of all of our writing sessions, Noah was never present.

Georgia adjusted her position, sitting more upright now. "As you may have assumed, I haven't told anyone about this. It's been a weight on my chest for years. The last time you wrote I told you I never saw Noah again. I did see him one last time."

My eyes widened in suspense. I saw Noah's do the same.

"I brought Noah down here often when he was little." She pointed to Noah, who was listening intently. "It's such a lovely place. Something about the water always brought peace to me. I had been sitting at this very table while Noah was just off to the park." She pointed to a set of swings connected with a long red slide just off to the right.

"I was sitting here drinking my coffee when I heard a familiar voice call my name. I turned abruptly to see Noah walking down the hill, well, staggering, I should say. I was in total shock. I hadn't seen him in five or six years. I looked over to see Noah Jr. He was oblivious for the moment on what was going on. He was sliding down the slide over and over." Georgia shook her head.

I watched Noah's eyes drift over to the small park Georgia was describing.

"He kept coming my way until he stumbled and fell to the ground. I grew furious instantly. My face was hot, and I began to cry. I walked over to him and grabbed his collar. The fumes of strong alcohol lifted from his clothes.

"'You bastard, you show up for the first time in years, and you're drunk!'

"He put his shaking hands over his eyes. 'Georgia, I came to tell you I love you, and I love Noah. I should have never left you. You were the only thing that ever made me truly happy.'

"I backed away, crossing my arms, and looked over toward Noah, who was now watching my every move while swinging on the swings. 'Get the hell out of here, Noah, now! I don't want my son seeing you, and especially like this. Come back in another five years sober.'

"I turned my back to him as he climbed back up the hill toward his yellow car. When he got to the top of the hill, he yelled, 'I love you, Georgia Harvest. I will always love you!'

"He waved to Noah, who had jumped off the swings and was waving back to the strange man. I turned to pick up Noah.

"'Momma, who was that?' he asked as I lifted him up. 'It was just an old friend, honey. Are you hungry yet?' I had started to gather all of our belongings to head home. I gave Noah five more minutes to go and play in the playground."

Noah interrupted. "I remember. I was running toward the swings. I turned around to see the yellow car flipping down the hill. It made a huge splash in the lake here. My mom was screaming, 'Noah! Noah!' As she ran toward the water, I remember three or four families running down the hill. Some men held my mother back as the car began to sink."

Georgia covered her mouth. "I was crying so loudly. The whole bottom of my dress was soaked. I had ran out as far as I could, but I wasn't even close. There was no way I would be able to save him." Georgia wiped a large tear from the corner of her eye.

"I loved him with all my heart. I was so mad at him, and those were the last words he heard."

Noah wrapped his arms around his mother. She was shaking a good bit. I scribbled her words across the blue lines.

Noah spoke up, "I remember sitting in the car at the top of the hill. You just sat in the driver's seat after buckling me in the back. I remember you crying and then turning around, smiling at me, asking me what I wanted for dinner. It was like nothing had happened. I remember seeing the police at the bottom of the hill pulling the car out. I was looking out the window, but your eyes were focused straight on the road." Noah looked at my hands as I jotted down every word and tried to capture every wrinkle of emotion in their faces.

"It never phased me that you would remember any of that. He was a good man, Noah. He lost sight of what was important for a while like we all do. He loved you, Noah, and he loved me."

Georgia ended the story. I told her I would add it on and I still wanted to send it out to publishers. Noah helped her up the hill, and I followed close behind. It was late now, a little after twelve.

Georgia turned to me before she got into Noah's truck. "What are you plans now?"

I slipped my tablet into my messenger bag. "I've saved up enough money. I'll be moving back to New York sometime soon."

Noah lifted his head as he pulled a gray tarp over the bed of his truck.

"There's just more opportunity there for writers, and I actually have an invitation for somewhere now, so it'll be good, you know?" I smiled at Georgia, trying to avoid Noah's eyes at all costs.

Georgia looked at me. "Well, congratulations, even though it sounds like you're consoling yourself about it." Georgia smirked. She could tell I wasn't set on the idea of leaving. "Come on, Noah, let's get on home. It's late now."

Noah got in the driver's seat, and just when I saw his lips purse as if he was about to say something to me, he waved good-bye, and they made their way out of the park. I wasn't far behind. At the fork in the road, Noah turned left toward their home, and I turned right toward mine.

I added the rest of the story as I promised Georgia. I sent a few copies out to publishing companies, and one was bound with ribbons and full of photographs I found that Georgia had given me of her travels. I was on my way to Georgia's to give that copy to her. I had spent most of the day packing boxes and marking them. My father had reluctantly agreed to drive me back to my old apartment, and my old Italian landlord had reluctantly agreed to me being a tenant again.

I got out of my car and felt the warm April sun on my face. A cool, lingering spring breeze shimmied through my hair. I walked up to the porch where Noah was sitting. He stood as I made my way up the stairs.

"Hey," he said with his hands in his pockets.

"Hey, I just wanted to drop all this off to your mom. It's all finished, now," I said, handing him the packet.

His rough hands touched mine, and then his eyes locked with mine. He licked his dry lips, and I saw a bead of sweat form at the corner of his forehead. "My mom's sleeping. She hasn't felt well at all today. I'll make sure I give it to her though."

I could feel the tension between us, it made me uncomfortable, so I said thank you and walked off the porch. "Hey, Meg, um, thanks for coming out so late last night. It meant a lot to my mom." Noah's hand was on the back of his neck.

"Yeah, no problem," I said as I hopped into my jeep and drove off. In the mirror I saw Noah watching my car until I was over the hill and I couldn't see him any longer and he couldn't see me.

I found myself down at the lake for hours. I sat at the pavilion Georgia had led me to the night before. I closed my eyes, picturing Noah running over to the swings as his father's car rolled down the hill. I saw Georgia scream and wade through the water as far out as she could go before the two men grabbed her and the wives of the men tried to calm her as a young Noah stood far off in silence. I felt a tear crawl down my cheek as I rubbed it away. I opened my eyes to the sound of a young boy climbing back up the red slide used by so many children in this town. Despite his mother's cries to be careful, he continued climbing up the slide over and over.

I had returned home to boxes that I had set up. I was still procrastinating packing. Of course it could all be done in one day, and I could leave the next, but I was holding off for something, some sign that I was meant to stay here. I would go to the lake everyday to see if Georgia or Noah might be there and make it seem as if by some ironic fate we ran into each other, but everyday I sat alone at the same pavilion Georgia had revealed the last of her story.

Today I made my way down the almost vertical hill and sat my messenger bag on the wooden table. I took out my notebook, as these days I was scribbling poems in the margins of the sheets of paper. After about an hour of being there, I was sharing my table with an older gentleman. He looked like he was in his late fifties or early sixties. He was tall and had gray hair under a fedora hat with a dark brown beard. He sat without a word as if he were sitting alone.

A few moments later he turned to me. "Excuse me for taking up room. I'd sit at another pavilion, but this one's special!" He clapped his hands together and smiled.

I smiled and welcomed him to do as he pleased. I turned my focus back down to my notebook. I couldn't shake off the feeling that I had met this man before. His face didn't seem familiar, but there was something about his voice.

Chapter 18

As I walked up the hill, leaving the man to himself, I couldn't shake the feeling that I had met him before. I got into my jeep and drove off. It was in the town center at the red light that it hit me like a ton of bricks. I made an illegal U-turn and headed back to the park in hopes of reaching the gentleman. Of course, despite my efforts, the mysterious man was gone. I didn't bother checking the other pavilions. I knew that was the only one he'd be at. It was the last place he saw his love.

This man's voice sat in my head all week long. I hadn't had any contact from Noah. In fact, he had stopped delivering with my father. He said he was busy all week. He wouldn't be free. I suspected it was his attempt to forget all about me by ignoring anything and anyone that reminded him of me. I didn't blame Noah.

I was staring at the boxes I had packed one evening when my father had come down looking for one of his old fishing books to loan a friend. It was spring, and fishing season was near.

My father noticed my gaze was not on the television screen. "So are you looking to move these soon?"

I shook my head. "I don't know what I'm doing right now, Dad. I've just got too many loose ends blowing around. I need to tie everything together, and when that's all done, I'll let you know if I need help moving those boxes. Hell, Dad, I might need help moving and changing my identity if I find any more puzzle pieces lying around, sitting at parks."

My father looked at me, fearful. "Parks? Is everything okay, Meaghan? You're not in any trouble, are you?"

I waved my hand at the thought. "No, Dad. There's just a lot on my mind right now. I've gone into detective mode." I laughed.

My father kissed my forehead and made his way back up the stairs, but not before sharing a bit of advice. "Meaghan, just don't go snooping around where your nose doesn't fit." He continued up the stairs.

I whispered, "It's beyond that point now."

"Meaghan, can you ring this young woman up?" My mother showed an elderly woman toward the register, who was holding a few necklace boxes and a pair of vintage gold bumble bee earrings. As I listened to her go on and on about how much she liked to dress up and how each necklace matched a dress she had, I saw the mysterious man from the park walking right past the window.

I quickly wrapped the woman's merchandise up and slammed it on the counter. I turned around the corner into the break room to grab my jacket and messenger bag. As I hurried out the door I yelled to my mother, "Break!"

The man had gotten into a small red Ford truck. I followed him to the lake and sat in my car to make sure I saw what I had seen in him before. When he finally sat down on the bench, I thought, You better be right, Meg.

I made my way down the hill toward the pavilion. I stepped on too many sticks and such to be unnoticed.

The man had turned to me, smiling. "My dear friend has returned." He lifted his cane and hit the corner of his hat, welcoming me to sit.

"Noah?" I said without hesitation.

I saw his wrinkles twist. His lips fell from the smile they once held. "Do I know you. I haven't heard my name spoken so softly in years. Who are you, young lady?"

I sat my messenger bag down on the table. "You are Noah Harvest, right?" I was still in disbelief of my discovery. It went against all my information.

"Who are you?" he demanded.

"I'm Meaghan. I'm a writer and a friend. I've only heard stories about you, and the only part I'm interested in is the end, because I see you here now, right in front of me. It doesn't add up with what I've written thus far."

I saw confusion in his face. I didn't feel I had time to go on and on about how I knew him. It was only moments later he said it for himself.

"Are you a friend of Georgia?" he asked earnestly. I saw hope in his eyes now, and I felt the adrenaline building in him from across the table.

"Yes! That's right. I am a friend of Georgia. I need you to tell me how it is possible I'm speaking with you right now."

He tapped his cane. "How'd you figure I was who you say I am?"

I smiled. "The first time I heard your voice a few days ago I couldn't shake the feeling that I knew you, that I had heard that same rumble in your voice before, and then it had hit me that night that you reminded me of Noah Harvest Jr. I have known him for some time now, and after I realized your voices I compared your jaw structures and your eyes and thought they were too unmistakably similar for you not to be Noah Harvest."

Noah Sr. sat for another moment before asking more questions. "Noah, is he well? I haven't seen him for years, and my sweet Georgia. How is she?"

I shook my head. "It's my turn to ask some questions. At the end of my story, I wrote that you had died at this very lake, and right down this hill, as a matter of fact. Your family has thought you've been dead all this time."

He looked back to the lake. "I never deserved the beautiful family I was given. This was the last place I saw them. I came that day after searching for weeks when I came up with nothing, so like an idiot I went out and had too much to drink. I drove up to this park here, and I couldn't believe it. I saw my Georgia sitting right here playing with our son. I tried to speak with her, but she asked me to leave. She had every right to. I had messed up too many times to be forgiven again. She told me she never wanted to see me again." Noah rubbed his right temple as if the memory was stuck there.

"I don't remember what happened after that. I was being pulled out of the water by men. They told me I wrecked and went into the lake. I called Georgia's name. One of the women told me she left already. They said she probably thought I was dead. I figured it was best she thought that. Her words of 'I never want to see you again' have always stuck in my mind."

I looked at Noah's sad face. "So that was it. You never made any attempt to at least let her know you were all right?" I asked, bewildered.

"No, I told you she never wanted to see me again, so I kept my distance, moved back to New Jersey with an old friend—" I cut him off.

"Sophia?" His head turned quickly. "No, no, she killed herself sometime before I made my way to Maine. I was staying with and old friend from high school. What do you know of Sophia anyway?"

"I know she was more than a friend." I locked eyes with him. I could see the aggression returning. "Look, I didn't come here to offend you."

Noah said quickly. "What the hell did you come for then?"

I crossed my hands and leaned in a little closer to him. "I have been writing for Georgia for some time now. I was dating Noah, and now our relationship is very rocky, if it's still existent anymore," I said, looking down. "I want to take you to Georgia. She's not doing well at all. In fact, I fear she won't be with us much longer. She has cancer."

Noah shook his head. "I can't after all this time. I know she wants nothing to do with me. She made that all very clear long ago."

"Yes, long ago. The last I heard her speak about you was that you were a good man and that she did love you, and as I've got it figured, neither you nor I have anything to lose."

I saw him stirring the idea in his mind.

I scribbled my phone number on a piece of notebook paper and sat it in front of him. "Just think about it. Georgia and Noah need to know you're still here," I said, leaving Noah Sr. alone once more.

I was certain Noah Sr. would have called me telling me he was ready to see his family again. On the contrary, two weeks had passed, and there was nothing. I had gone to the pavilion days in a row without seeing him. I would wait for hours on end with no trace of the man anywhere. I began to lose hope.

I was sitting in my bedroom flipping through the channels until my irritation level built up to the brim. I was doing nothing with all the new information I had. I was in purgatory again, just sitting. I grabbed my messenger bag and slid into my flip-flops—it was just warm enough to wear them—and I headed to the park.

When I turned into the old black iron gate, I saw a familiar red Ford truck parked at the top of the hill. I parked behind it, and when I got out I noticed another familiar truck parked in front of it. It was Noah's truck. I bounced down the hill toward the pavilion where I was shocked to see Noah Sr. sitting across from Noah Jr. I was filled with anger.

Noah Jr. turned around and stood at the sight of me. I welcomed him with a hard slap to the face.

"What the hell is this? Is this some kind of game you two have got going on me?"

Noah grabbed my waist, and Noah Sr. pleaded with me to sit.

"Now look, writer, you'll get your answers as long as you sit down and listen. People come here for peace. Don't disrupt it," Noah Sr. spoke sternly.

I sat a few hands away from Noah Jr., who was rubbing his left cheek, which was stained red.

Noah Sr. began, "I thought about what you said. I've got nothing more to lose. I wanted to meet Noah and

Georgia again. I just didn't know how to go about it all. I thought Noah here would be more understanding with my presence than Georgia. Like you, she's got a sharp tongue." He shook his head, smiling. "I looked my boy up, and I asked him to meet me today at this pavilion. We hadn't spoken much when you showed up."

I stood in anger again. "Well, excuse me for interrupting your meeting. I'll be leaving now."

Noah Jr. grabbed my arm. "It sucks when someone you trust is hiding a secret from you, doesn't it, Meg?" I saw anger in his eyes as well.

"What, so this is some sort of revenge? Some sort of screw me over?"

Noah and I exchanged a few rude words before Noah Sr. stood, and we both sat again.

"My God, this isn't about you two or myself. This is about Georgia, the woman who has been good to us all. Now we have to find some way to give her a peace of mind, and unfortunately I believe she won't have one until you two are on good terms, and as for myself, I would like to speak with her soon, not too soon, but soon enough."

Noah waited for a response of agreement. I sat like a child with my arms crossed, and Noah was staring at me, smiling. I couldn't help but smile back.

Noah Sr. laughed. "Well, then it's settled!"

My mind was racing that evening. We had devised half a plan to see Georgia. I was more than nervous. I hadn't seen her for some time now. I wasn't sure how she would look, and more importantly, how she would react to Noah's presence. I feared it would take a toll on her failing health.

Noah Jr. insisted everything would work out fine. His positive energy was the only thing keeping this mission active. However, when we departed I could see the uneasiness in his eyes. Noah walked me to my car after our discussion with Noah Sr.

"So I bet you were surprised to hear his voice."

We both laughed.

Noah gripped the back of his neck. "All these years I thought he was gone, you know? And then just out of the blue." He looked shocked.

"You weren't mad?" I inquired.

"No, how could I be? I respected his decision to stay away from my mother. It's what she asked of him. And as far as him leaving my mother, he apologized sincerely. That was a burden he's had to live with. I forgave him."

I lifted my brow. "Good. I'm very happy for you to be reunited and all, you know, Noah," I began as I walked to my car. "The only reason I didn't tell you about your mother's illness was because I respected her enough not to, even if it meant hiding something from you. Where's my forgiveness?"

Noah stood silent, and I drove off.

Chapter 19

I overheard my father a few days later telling my mother he was glad to have Noah back on delivery. "He's a strong guy, good to have around."

I felt my lips curl into a smile. I was bound to be seeing him around more often. I had met up with Noah Sr. at the pavilion two days in a row to discuss how he could visit Georgia without making too much of a disruption.

"Noah, anyway you do this is going to be disruption. I mean, Jesus, she's thought you've been dead all this time."

Noah put his head in his hands. "Every time we talk about this I feel I can't do it. I just need to see her one last time to explain everything, to tell her I love her even if she doesn't accept it. It's all I want."

I grabbed Noah's worn hands. "You can do this. We'll just have to brief with Noah Jr. and find out when it's best to see her." I smiled, trying to uplift Noah's doubts, even though I had many of my own.

I walked around my room from the steps to the television and back and forth, running everything through my mind. I hadn't seen Georgia for quite some time. I wasn't sure how she felt about me, and I wasn't sure how she'd feel about me bringing Noah Sr. back into her life. I stopped in the middle of my pacing to answer the knock at my door. When I opened the door, Noah Jr. was walking back to his truck.

I yelled in confusion, "Noah? Did you knock?"

He was rubbing the back of his neck as he did often in awkward situations. "Um, yeah. I did. I didn't think you were home, so I was going to leave."

I laughed. "You only knocked once. I got to the door as fast as I could. Did you want to talk or something?" I asked, smiling hopefully.

"Yeah, if you've got some time."

"Of course, come in," I said, walking back into my room, waiting for him to make his way in.

My heart was pounding from the moment I saw him standing outside. When he closed the door and sat on my futon beside me, I thought he had to notice my heart beating out of my chest, just as obvious as in the old cartoons.

"Is everything all right?" I asked.

"Well, it's as right as it can be. I wanted to apologize for yelling at you that night at the hospital. I'm sure you could understand I was very upset. My whole world was spinning. I'm not sure of anything these days. My mom is dying, and there's nothing I can do about it. I just found out my father, who I thought was nonexistent, is alive and breathing and that we have more in common than I would have ever known!" Noah's voice was rising. He was clearly distraught.

"All this time I feel like everything is just whirling around me, and every time I stop it's because I see you. You're my fixed point, and it kills me not talking to you. At first it was easy because I was pissed at the world, but after a few days, especially that night at the pavilion with my mother, God, you looked so beautiful. I just want to have you there to hold every night, and I want to see your smile every morning. You were the best thing I've ever had to hold close. I was an idiot. Can we start over?"

The sincerity in his eyes drove me on top of him. We kissed. We laughed. We cuddled.

"Noah?" I whispered in the night.

"Mhmm," he moaned.

"I love you."

He rolled over to me, kissing my forehead. "I love you too, Meaghan." He held me against his warm chest the rest of this night.

The next morning I opened my eyes slightly to him putting his boots on and fiddling his keys. He scribbled on a piece of scrap paper on my desk and shut the door quietly behind him. I shut my eyes for a little longer until my mind refused to let me go back to sleep. I walked over to my metal desk and slowly raised the paper to my eyes and read it aloud.

Meg,

I'm sorry for leaving so early. I had a gut feeling I should go check on my mom. I'll see you this evening. I want you to come over for dinner. I'll call you later.

Love,
Noah

I put the letter in the blue wastebasket to the right of my futon. I yawned and hopped into the shower, washing off the sweat that clung to my skin from last night. It was nearing eight or so, and I was sitting on my futon wearing a long blue skirt and a white tank top waiting for Noah.

I was beyond nervous to see Georgia. I figured she'd be joining us for dinner. I checked my hair once more when I saw the reflection of his headlights pulling in. I was out the door and in his truck before he got out.

"Look at you." He smiled.

We didn't speak much until we walked on the porch. I sensed he was nervous. I had anticipated Georgia looking ill.

He turned to me when he opened the front door. "She doesn't look the same as a few months ago."

I kissed his cheek. "She's still Georgia."

Noah entered the kitchen first. I smelt the roasted chicken and potatoes. Georgia was smiling at the table. She had a black walker to the right of her. Her hair was scarce.

"Hey, Meaghan, you clean up nice for a writer." She laughed as I made my way over to kiss her cheek.

"So do you, Georgia."

Noah brought green beans and biscuits to the table. I reached for the sweet tea. Georgia didn't eat much. Noah and I spoke most of the night.

At one point when we were cleaning up the dishes, she said, "I'm glad you two are getting along. Nothing makes me happier than seeing you happy, Noah."

"I know, Mom." Georgia went into the back room, which used to be the greenhouse.

Noah had transformed it into a bedroom for Georgia so she didn't have to climb the stairs in pain. Noah joined me in the living room with a beer.

"Dinner was delicious. You are quite the cook, more than I can say for myself."

Noah shrugged. "I got most of it from my mom. The rest I just observed from others. It's not a hard thing to pick up, well, for me anyway. It sort of comes naturally, like writing to you."

I smiled. "I never thought of it that way. Your mom, she's looks good."

Noah huffed. "No, she doesn't, Meg. If you're going to comfort me, at least be realistic with me."

I grabbed his hand. "She's still smiling as bright as a few months ago. She looks great to me."

Noah kissed my forehead. "I told my father we would find a good time to bring him in here. I just don't know when that would be. Sometimes I think she could handle it. Other days I look at her and think it would kill her. He wants to see her so bad. I just don't know how to tell her, how to prepare her for something like that. How would you handle seeing a man you loved after all these years, after all this time thinking he was dead?"

I turned my head sharply as I heard a shuffle behind the wall and covered my mouth as Georgia's body turned the corner.

"What the hell are you talking about, Noah Jr. Harvest?"

Noah stood, spilling his beer, and quickly picked it up and put it on the coffee table. "I didn't know you were up—"

Georgia angrily cut him off. "Why are you in here talking about your father?"

"Ma, I—"

"Noah Harvest, don't lie to me. What are you talking about?"

I saw Noah was speechless. Utters can from his mouth while Georgia bit into him.

Finally I blurted out the words he was searching for. "Noah's alive!" And then my blurt went into a long paragraph of information. I wasn't sure when it was going to stop. "He's alive. He never drowned at the lake like you thought. He just stayed away all these years because that's what you asked of him. Noah and I have met up with him a few times, and he wants to see you, Georgia. I swear he is sincere in meeting up with you. We were going to tell you. We were just waiting for the right moment." I froze and let out a long breathe.

Noah was looking at me and then turned slowly to see his mother's face. We waited for Georgia to speak. It felt like an eternity before she said anything and what she said was unexpected.

"Take me to him."

Noah helped Georgia into the back of my Jeep. He rushed back inside the house for me and to get a light blanket for his mother.

"You ready for this?"

I smiled and nodded my head. I wasn't prepared for anything. I just wanted to write everything that unfolded. He saw me reach for a loose pen and pad from his desk.

"You're a natural." He laughed.

I had called Noah Sr. to meet us at the pavilion right away. He said he'd be there with hesitation in his voice. Noah and I exchanged worried glances as we were first to get there, and an hour had passed with no sign of him. None of us had spoken since we left the house. Georgia was sitting on the bench with her quilt wrapped tightly around her. The late spring breeze lingered. Summer was approaching quickly.

Noah brushed up against me and whispered, "Where is he?"

I shook my head worriedly. "He sounded hesitant on the phone. He's been rightfully nervous, you know that. He knows this is his chance. He'll show. It's only a matter of when."

As if on cue headlights shone bright on top of the hill. I looked back at Georgia, who now sat straight up, pulling her hat down tightly atop of her head. She was nervous also. I felt I was watching a first date behind the scenes. Noah Jr. sat down beside his mother.

I welcomed Noah Sr. halfway down the hill. "I didn't think you were going to show."

"You knew I would or you would have been the one to lead them back on home." He smirked, and we continued toward the pavilion.

We were fifty feet in front of Georgia when she yelled, "You stop right there, Noah Harvest."

Noah and I came to an abrupt stop as Georgia had instructed.

"Why are you here?"

Noah took a step forward, and Georgia yelled again, "Stay where you are! Why are you here all of a sudden?"

Noah nervously rubbed the top of his cane. "Georgia, I wanted to see you. I wanted to tell you I love you."

Georgia laughed diabolically. "I watched you tumble into this lake. I couldn't bare the sight of those men pulling your lifeless body out of the water. I thought you were dead!" Georgia's voice cracked. A shadow was cast on her face. I couldn't make out if she was crying or not.

Noah held his hat in his hand for a moment. "Georgia, can I come closer and talk to you?"

"I'm not the same woman, Noah. I don't look the same these days." Georgia's head lowered.

Noah stepped slowly forward. The moonlight made Georgia's pale face clear now. Noah slipped her hat off, revealing her nearly bald head. She gasped.

"You still are just as beautiful as when I first saw you."

Georgia smiled wide as I felt tears building up in my eyes.

Noah moved closer, sitting beside her. "And that smile, just as bright as the stars."

Georgia touched Noah's face. "Noah, is it true? Is this really you?"

Noah wrapped his arms around Georgia's small body. "I'm here, Georgia. I promise I'll be here from now on if you want me here."

Georgia and Noah hugged tightly. I wiped a tear of happiness from my cheek. Noah Jr. was crying also. It was the first time I had seen that side of him. We all sat under the moonlight for hours laughing, smiling, and enjoying the each other's company. We all returned to Georgia's home for the night. I entangled in Noah's strong arms, staring at the ceiling smiling. I felt free of guilt, free of pain, free of negativity. I felt complete for the first time in my life.

None of us left the house for days. We took tons of pictures. I wanted to capture every moment. I knew there were few left. Each picture was titled, "Georgia Harvest Challenge" like the ones before.

Noah Sr. shared his stories over time. He had gotten work as a logger for a while, and then he was a busser in a small family restaurant. He spoke about Sophia's suicide, about how they both grew miserable with each other, because the love was never there. After he moved out she shot herself.

"We pretended for some time that we loved each other. It wasn't genuine. The only woman I ever thought about was my Georgia." Noah reached for her frail hand to hold.

Noah Jr. and I grew closer than we had been before our feud. We spent everyday together. He held me every night, and we endlessly made love.

Georgia called my name one evening while I was in the kitchen pouring some tea. I slid the old barn door across, which Noah creatively refurbished for the bedroom door.

"Did you call for me?" I asked.

Georgia welcomed me to a floral chair in the corner. "I wanted to ask you something. Do you love my Noah?"

I smiled. "I wouldn't be here with him if I didn't."

Georgia asked again, "Do you love my Noah?" I saw the seriousness in her eyes. I didn't like the feeling in the room any longer.

"Yes, I do love him."

Georgia smiled brightly. "Meaghan, I knew from the moment you pulled into my driveway that you were a special girl. I knew my son would be attracted to you, because you are so different. You are genuine, you are beautiful, you are independent, you are a wonderful writer, and you are my best friend."

I felt tears sitting at the brim of my lids like swimmers waiting to dive down my face. I wanted to leave the room. "Georgia, let me go get Noah." I stood.

She waved her hand and set it down quickly as if she was lifting fifty-pound weights. "No, please sit. I have more to tell you, and I know you are the only one who will understand and let me speak."

I sat.

"Meaghan, I will die tonight. I can feel it, but I could not be more at peace. You brought me back the love of my life, you brought my son and I closer, and you wrote my story. I am so grateful to have known you, and I must ask one more favor of you."

My tears were at a constant flow now.

Georgia smiled all the while she spoke, as if to ease the twisting I felt in my heart. "Meaghan, I need you to love Noah everyday I'm not here. I need you to be his paperweight now. I need you to help him get through all the fears he'll have after I'm gone. I need you to be there for him and guide him as you have done for me. I need you to explain to my men that I could not have been happier, more at ease than in this moment. I need you to tell them to enjoy each other's company every single day. Can you do this for me?"

I lifted my heavy head to look at Georgia's glowing face. Her bright smile could fool anyone into thinking that she was healthy and well. "Yes, I will, Georgia. I will," I said with a long sigh. "Georgia, where will I find the strength for all this?"

Georgia laughed. "Why do you think I called you in here? You are strong already, Meaghan. You were born with strength."

I leaned over Georgia, squeezing her tightly and whispering into her ear, "You are one hell of a woman. I love you."

It wasn't much longer when Georgia's small chest stopped lifting. It's a strange thing to hear someone's last breath. It's a sound that could silence Time Square on New Year's Eve, like the first gunshot in a war. Time slows. A minute feels like a lifetime. You stand frozen until something jolts you back into reality. I saw a tear slowly fall to my hand, and then I watched the door slide across, and when Noah's eyes met mine, he fell to his knees, submerging himself in tears of anger and sadness.

Noah Sr. came to the door hurriedly at the sound of Noah's cries. His cane fell hard on the cold gray tile. He put his hand over his heart and sobbed, whispering, "My sweet Georgia."

And she was gone, like a quick breeze in the hot summer night.

Epilogue

Nine months after Georgia's death, I received an e-mail from a woman whose name was Sylvia.

> I was wondering if you were still interested in having your story published, because I am very interested in publishing it!

Excitement ran up my vocal cords, and I screamed at the top of my lungs in the kitchen one afternoon. Noah Jr. and Sr. rushed in, demanding to know what the chaos was about. When I informed them that Georgia's story would soon be sitting on the shelves, they embraced each other and clapped. We were all filled with joy.

Noah turned to me. "Thank you, now everyone will get to know a little about how incredible Georgia Harvest was." He smiled.

———

Three months after Georgia's story was published and made it to the bestseller's list, Noah proposed to me at the pavilion one evening. The wooden picnic table was centered with tea light candles and peonies. Shortly after we ate a small meal he packed, he made his way over to my side of the table, and the instant he got on his knee, I was in tears, smiling the rest of the night and days to follow.

Two weeks later we were married in Georgia's back yard. Her beautiful garden was in full bloom, and my parents and Noah Sr. had set up a big, beautiful white tent for the reception. Pink and white Chinese lanterns hung from the top with dangling white lights to keep the dancing and such going until after dark.

Georgia's wedding ring was now on my ring finger, and I was officially inducted into the Harvest family. We had taken a small vacation to California, visiting the beaches and Yosemite park.

While in Cali, fate had brought two boys to me whose names were Tyler and Tobias. When I entered a crowded corner store and learned of their names, I asked them if their mother's name was perhaps Candice. When they shook their heads yes, I revealed in the connection that brought us together. Tyler and Tobias smiled and exchanged looks with each other, and Tobias pulled a hard copy of The Story of Georgia Harvest from behind the counter.

I was informed that his mother remarried a lawyer, and they lived happy lives until her passing three years ago. She spoke often throughout her life about Miss Georgia and how she had inspired her to keep going. Tobias allowed Noah and I to have dinner with his brother Tyler and his wife, who was shocked to see me when we arrived at a local Italian restaurant. Her name was Cassie, and we shook hands and pretended we had never met before. The world is a small place.

When we returned home, I began working on another book. The process would be interrupted with the pregnancy of our daughter, who we named Georgia Liana Harvest. Whether or not you believe in reincarnation, our daughter had Georgia's bright smile and her delicate eyes.

Georgia would grow to be a teacher at the Franklin Elementary School down the road. She would marry a creative writing teacher by the name of Jake Shepherd.

Noah Sr. lived with us for five joyful years, spending most of his days with his beautiful granddaughter until his passing. He was buried beside Georgia. Their tombstones read, "Eternal lovers."

My brother Bryan finished school and became an architect. He opened his own successful construction company here in Franklin. Later, he met a real woman at the Corner Café who was dedicated to loving him loyally. She was a new barista from Nevada. They were married shortly after they met and are happily together today with two boys and expecting a baby girl.

My father retired from the moving business, spending the rest of his days with his granddaughter on his lap watching hunting shows. He died late one night peacefully in his sleep of natural causes.

My mother is widowed, spending her days at the jewelry shop, the place she had always enjoyed being at.

Noah took over my father's moving business and worked diligently everyday until retiring two years ago. Our love for each other grew as strong as steel over the years, and to this day four months after his death, I feel him around me. I feel him pulling me close when I lie in bed at night, and I hear his whispers of "I love you."

I spend my time scribbling words on paper day after day after day. I have had two other books published since Georgia's. Her story, however, will always be the greatest thing I've ever written.

Georgia's tradition of taking pictures everyday has been passed on and continued throughout my family. Bins of pictures are stored around the house. I find myself looking at them often, smiling. If Georgia had taught me anything at all, it was most importantly to spend the greatest part of my time with the ones I love.

As I finish my entry, I'm lying in the guest room Noah had built for Georgia long ago. My daughter is sitting in the floral chair in the corner where I sat. My last breath is escaping like a quick breeze in the summer night.

Lightning Source UK Ltd.
Milton Keynes UK
UKOW07f1934141214

243121UK00013B/151/P